TO CAPTURE A HEART

When Gill Madison visited the beautiful Malaysian island, Langkawi, at the end of a backpacking holiday, she knew she would love to spend more time there. Being on the spot for an offer of a 'Girl Friday' job on board a pleasure boat seems too good an offer to turn down, especially when the skipper is as handsome as Bart Lawson. However, Gill soon discovers that it isn't all to be plain sailing.

KAREN ABBOTT

TO CAPTURE A HEART

Complete and Unabridged

LINFORD
Leicester

First published in Great Britain in 2006

First Linford Edition
published 2006

British Library CIP Data

Abbott, Karen
    To capture a heart.—Large print ed.—
Linford romance library
1. Love stories
2. Large type books
I. Title
823.9'14 [F]

    ISBN 1–84617–490–2

Published by
F. A. Thorpe (Publishing)
Anstey, Leicestershire

Set by Words & Graphics Ltd.
Anstey, Leicestershire
Printed and bound in Great Britain by
T. J. International Ltd., Padstow, Cornwall

This book is printed on acid-free paper

1

Gill Madison sat on the capstan at the end of the jetty at Kuah on the Malaysian island of Langkawi and gazed out to sea. A large rucksack sat by her feet, looking more travel-stained than its owner. Her tough walking shoes dangled one at each side, tied on by their laces, and were replaced on her feet by a pair of dainty, strapped sandals that revealed the incongruous normal pale skin of feet that had been protected from the sun's relentless rays for the duration of her backpacking holiday.

The sea was as bright a blue as she had ever seen, reflecting the equally bright blue cloudless sky. The sun bore down with a blistering heat. Gill was glad of the sun hat she wore, covering the crown of her long blonde hair.

The ferryboat ought to have been

here by now and she should have been on her way, albeit reluctantly, to Penang, just off the Malaysian mainland, from where she was due to fly on to Kuala Lumpur.

Impatiently, she looked at her watch, her blue eyes widening in disbelief. The fingers had moved on only five minutes since the last time she had looked, and that felt like at least twenty minutes ago! She held it to her ear, shaking it, as if that would suddenly make it spring into life, but didn't.

She frowned as she stared at the dial once more and immediately leaped to her feet, casting her glance around anxiously. No wonder there were no officials looking as though they were expecting the imminent arrival of the ferryboat from Thailand, nor any would-be passengers drifting along the pier and forming a queue! Apart from a number of privately-owned yachts tied up at the jetty and a few tourists strolling along admiring the scenery, the area was deserted except for herself, now feeling conspicuous with her ungainly backpack at her side.

She had no idea what time it was. Oh, why today, of all days? Her shoulders slumped in despair as she realised that she had missed the ferry, and there wasn't another until lunchtime of the following day.

The holiday group she had been with, backpacking around northern Malaysia and southern Thailand, had already split up and her fellow travellers were making their way back to their various homeland countries. Gill had intended to move on to the Malaysian capital, Kuala Lumpur, for a week or so and then travel to the south and spend a few weeks on and around Singapore island, before returning to England at the end of the year to take up a teaching job near Manchester, after a four-month sabbatical between jobs.

A dispute at the airport in Thailand had thrown her plans into disarray when she had been informed that the plane she was booked on to fly to

Penang, and then to Kuala Lumpur, had been delayed for twenty-four hours at the last minute. A quick study of the ferry timetable had inspired her to take the ferryboat instead, stopping off at Langkawi in order to see the lovely island that she had heard described.

'But you must still fly to Kuala Lumpur from Penang,' the harassed official at the enquiry desk had told her. 'I cannot change your flight to depart from Langkawi. That flight is already fully booked.'

'That's OK!' Gill had assured him gaily. 'I'll get a cheap overnight stay and catch the same ferry the following day.'

The official had re-stamped her airline ticket with tonight's date, making it clear that it was up to her to be there on time, and Gill had blithely taken the airport bus to the ferry port. But that was yesterday.

She had spent the afternoon and evening in and around Kuah. This morning she had spent some of her remaining money on a whistle-stop minicab tour of the island. The beauty of Langkawi had touched her heart. Maybe she was to spend at least one more day here!

The flight from Penang was due to take off later that evening and Gill now knew she had no chance of making it, not even if the ferry miraculously appeared right there and then! It would have been a tight enough schedule to keep even if she had been on the long-departed ferry. There had been no leeway for a missed connection!

With a slight pang in her stomach, she knew she was stranded in a foreign land with no immediate means of continuing her holiday as planned. She doubted that she would get a refund for her missed flight. She chewed her lower lip. What on earth could she do? Maybe she could get some sort of job here on Langkawi to tide her over a few days. But where to start? It must be late afternoon and the daily rainfall would be upon them soon.

'Hey! You, girl! Look lively! I haven't got all day!'

The masculine voice penetrated Gill's gloomy thoughts and she turned round to see who was calling out, and to whom. Tied to a capstan a few metres behind her was a two-masted catamaran. Its twin hulls were white, with a fine blue line painted half a metre or so above the waterline. The sails, at present, were at half-mast. One sail was white and the other turquoise blue with the emblem of a white flying horse. Was it aptly named, she wondered, glancing at the yacht's name, Pegasus, painted just above the blue line. Did the boat indeed fly over the waves?

A tall, lanky, sun-bronzed man stood, legs apart, on the deck, his hands on his hips. His eyes were directed at Gill, or someone close behind her. She looked over her shoulder but could see nothing but the sea. She turned back again. He couldn't mean her, could he? She didn't know him from Adam. His dark hair hung untidily over one eye and even as she noticed this, he pushed a hand through it, in an attempt to bring it under control.

'Well, are you coming or not?' the man demanded. 'As I said, I haven't got all day. The wind is just right and I want to be off before it drops.'

Gill took a hesitant step forward, her hand automatically looping through the straps of her backpack. Her mind whirled as she slowly made her way towards the boat, her eyes fixed on the man's face. Who was he? Why did he think she had any connection with him? She stopped about half a metre away from the edge of the jetty.

'What's your name?' she asked suspiciously.

'Bart Lawson. What's yours?'

'Gill Madison.'

'Well, Gill Madison, are you coming on board or not? You are from the agency, aren't you? The hired hand I'm expecting?'

Gill glanced down the pier, thinking

quickly. There was obviously no-one else applying for the job, and it would give her bed and board for a few days until she could sort something out! Even so, how did she know she could trust him? What if he were simply out to pick up just any girl he might see and whisk her away to a desert island or to some far-off place where the white-slave trade was still in operation?

She looked him up and down again.

'I could be!' she retorted. 'They didn't mention wages or anything, such as where I'm to sleep and . . . er . . . time off and such like.'

'Your wage is your food and lodgings, and a lump sum bonus at the end of the season, if you're still with us. You'll sleep in the rear cabin, and time off when the work is done! Any more questions?'

Bart studied her, his hands on his hips, perfectly balanced on the softly swaying deck. Her eyes were almost almond shaped and as blue as the sea behind her, and, although they were now avidly assessing him, they seemed to promise fun and laughter. He doubted that she had been sent from the agency. She was too surprised by his call, but he felt that he wanted to get to know her. There was something appealing about her, something that tugged somewhere deep inside him.

Ah, well! Maybe it wasn't to be! He turned to a young Malaysian boy who was watching from the engine house.

'Cast off, Wak!'

The boy jumped on to the pier and bent down to unwind the first rope that held the boat captive. He gathered it into his hands, tossed it on board as the bow drifted away from the jetty and moved along the pier to the rope at the stern. When it was loose in his hands, he prepared to leap back on board with it.

'OK! See you, babe!' Bart called, saluting farewell with a casual wave.

'No! No! Wait! I'm coming!' Gill yelled, galvanised into action by the prospect of being left stranded on the pier.

At least he was European, English even, though it was difficult to tell. She swung her backpack towards him.

'Here! Catch!'

With barely a pause, she then leaped forward herself, aiming to land where there was a short break in the knee-high rail that ran around the outer edge of the deck. Bart held out his hand and caught her neatly as her feet slipped from under her as they hit the deck. She grabbed at him wildly, clutching hold of his firm arms. For a second or two, their bodies clung to each other.

Her heart was thudding rapidly in her chest, and it was quite a pleasant experience. He had a body to die for!

'Welcome aboard!'

Bart grinned down at her. His lips, parted in a smile, revealed perfectly-formed white teeth and Gill felt quite heady as she raised her eyes to meet his, wishing her heart would calm down.

Surely he could feel its frantic pounding.

'I didn't expect you to fall for me quite so soon!' Bart teased, looking as though he was enjoying the impromptu embrace.

'Don't flatter yourself!' Gill snapped, feeling at a distinct disadvantage. 'If you will let me go, I'm sure I can manage on my own now.'

'Sure thing, honey!'

He released his hold on her and glanced down at the strappy sandals on her feet.

'Pretty though they are, you'll find it safer to be barefoot on deck. The soles of your feet will grip the surface more securely than any footwear. We keep our shoes in that box under the seat in the wheelhouse and take it with us whenever we go ashore.'

He stepped along the deck, saying over his shoulder, 'Dump your bag in the cabin and get ready to help Wak with the lines.'

Gill halted.

'Pardon?'

'Help Wak. That is what you're here for, isn't it?'

Gill swallowed. She hadn't really taken it in. She knew absolutely nothing about boats! Well, she couldn't admit that, could she?

'Fine!' she said briefly.

The boat had already drifted away from the quayside and Bart had seated himself in the high cabin where the steering-wheel was housed. He reached forward and turned a switch and a powerful engine sprang into life.

That was a relief, Gill thought. At least they weren't totally dependent on the sails, the manoeuvring of which was a total mystery to her. She deposited her backpack in the main cabin, swaying with the unaccustomed motion. She joined Wak near the back of the boat, the stern, she reminded herself, pleased to recall its nautical term. The stern and the . . .

'Bow!' she remembered aloud.

'Miss?' Wak queried.

Gill grinned at him.

'Nothing. I was just practising some nautical terms.'

She gestured with her arms, indicating the mast, sails and deck area.

'I'm not used to boats . . . er . . . of this class, Wak. You'll have to show me what to do.'

'Yes, miss.'

He was a nice-looking Indian Malay, with short dark hair, olive skin, very slender and of medium height. He looked to be in his mid-to-late teens.

'What do I do?' she asked, watching as he hauled in a small buffer that had been fastened to the outer edge of the boat where it had been between the boat and jetty.

'Pull in the other fenders,' he told her, 'and stow them away like this.'

He placed the fender in a recess let into the side of the hull and Gill moved along to the next one and did the same with that. There were two more to do and she willingly drew them on board and stowed them away. She would do all right if all the work were going to be this easy!

Well-pleased with herself, she braced her legs to counterbalance the movement of the deck as the catamaran surged forward. She stood gazing ahead with her hands on her hips. There was a short area of decking the full width of the boat in front of the engine house. She could imagine lying there in the warm sunshine, sipping a cool drink. In front of that were two areas of rope netting, each about four metres square, with a centre metal strut to strengthen them, covering the space at the bows between the twin hulls. Another sun-bathing area, she supposed, wondering how much time she would be able to spend there.

They were clear of the boats moored close to the land and the twin hulls of the catamaran were slicing through the calm water, sending up refreshing sprays of sea water. It was beautiful!

'Ahoy, there!' Bart's voice reached her. 'Work time!'

'What now?' Gill asked, stepping towards the engine house.

Her hair whipped forward across her smiling lips and she drew it back with her fingers as she looked enquiringly at Bart.

'Time to run up the sails. Ever done that?'

His right eyebrow rose quizzically and Gill wondered if he could see her for the landlubber that she was. It was too soon for such an admission. He might turn right around and dump her back on the landing stage!

'Er, not on a boat of this size,' she said quite truthfully, mentally crossing her fingers because of the unspoken deception.

'Right! Watch, listen and learn!'

He switched off the engine and slipped out of the raised cabin. He snapped a few orders to Wak and the young Malaysian boy leaped to do his bidding. Between the two of them, they quickly raised the sails and adjusted the ropes, fastening them securely, working

15

with a well-practised rhythm that Gill could only marvel to watch, quite certain that she would never be able to master it herself! Bart had her fasten the occasional figure-of-eight loop and watched her appraisingly.

'You haven't done much of this, have you?' he ventured at length.

'Not a great deal,' she agreed, hastily adding, 'but I'm a quick learner!'

'You'd better be! What exactly can you do?'

He towered over her, his eyes slightly narrowed as he awaited her answer. Gill sucked in her breath, refusing to meet his penetrating gaze. She wondered fleetingly if this were time for complete honesty. She was facing towards the stern and she could still see land. Too soon, she reckoned.

'I can cook!' she said swiftly, smiling winsomely. 'And I'm good at cleaning. Oh, and lots of things, really,' she added hopefully.

'A regular Girl Friday, eh?' Bart suggested with a wry grin.

'Mm, something like that. Will that do?'

'Didn't the agency tell you what my requirements are?'

'N . . . no, not really. A sort of Jack-of-all-trades to help with cruises?' she asked rather than stated, thinking it a likely idea.

To her relief, Bart was nodding.

'I've been running cruises for two years from Kuah and Awana, working as a sub-contractor with a larger enterprise. This year, I've got an arrangement with a hotel in the northwest that I will do day cruises around the island, exclusively for their guests. It's a great opportunity for me.'

He paused and looked at her appraisingly. Gill couldn't read what he was thinking. The idea appealed to her, and it was true about her being a quick learner. She would try her hand at anything within reason! And Singapore could wait for another year!

She held her breath, hoping Bart would agree to keep her on. He looked at her soberly as he weighed her in the balance.

'I need a loyal crew. This is my grandfather's boat and he says that if I make a go of it this season, the boat's mine. I've got to make it pay and I've got to be able to renew the contract next year, otherwise, the deal's off. Do you reckon you can pull your weight? If not, this is the time to say so and I'll take you back ashore.'

2

Gill swallowed hard. She would hate to be the cause of this young man failing in his enterprise. Would he stand a better chance with someone who was used to boats? But no-one else had turned up, had they? The agency had obviously let him down. It was her or no-one, and, she could see a glance that the catamaran needed at least a three-man crew to run effectively with passengers on board.

Pushing aside her doubts, she nodded eagerly and, after a slight hesitation, held out her hand with confident frankness.

'I'm right with you. I'll do my best.'

'You're only on trial,' Bart warned her, as he took her hand in his. 'I need a hard-working crew. The only passengers I'll carry are the paying ones!'

'That's OK! Like I said, I'll do my best.'

They grinned at each other, both satisfied with the deal.

Gill felt suddenly light-headed and filled with exhilaration. Her original itinerary hadn't included a prolonged sea-cruise but it was something she was sure she would enjoy and, although she hadn't done any sailing to date, she was good at outdoor sports.

Her hand was still held in Bart's firm grasp and her senses reeled at the physical contact with him, confirming her instant attraction to him, but this was to be a working relationship and she didn't want to jeopardise that. She laughed self-consciously and gently pulled her hand away.

'So, what happens next?' she asked.

'We're sailing halfway round the island to Datai Bay at the edge of the Andaman Sea and we'll drop anchor there for the night.'

He glanced at Wak who was steering the catamaran competently, heading between two tiny islands.

'We're going seaward of the smaller

islands,' he explained. 'When we have passengers, we usually take the inland route as it's more picturesque, but this route will be much faster. How well do you know Langkawi?'

'Not very well,' Gill admitted, her gaze travelling beyond Bart, revelling in the force of the wind against her face.

The sea was a bit wilder out here and the boat dipped and rose over the waves in a rhythmic motion.

'I've been backpacking around Northern Malaysia and Thailand and a few members of the group I was with had been here a year or so ago. They sang its praises and I wanted to see it.'

Being normally truthful by nature, she only managed to bite back at the last moment how she had missed the ferry and was thus here by accident. Instead, she turned to smile at Bart.

'Now, I'll be seeing it from the sea instead of backpacking around.'

'Oh, you'll see some of it from the land. Some cruises include time spent ashore and I find most tourists appropriate a guide. You'll have to gen up on local folklore.'

He turned to look at Wak.

'Are you all right at the helm, Wak? Good. Come into the cabin, Gill. I'll show you where to stow your gear and then I'll show you a map of the island and explain a bit about where we'll be going tomorrow.'

Gill followed him down the few steps beside the wheelhouse into the main cabin. It was about three metres square in area, with padded bench-type seats along the right hand side and part of the two ends. A table, covered with maps, took centre place and a small kitchen was to the left hand side. Gill poked her head inside.

'Not enough room to swing a cat!' she commented humorously. 'How on earth do you manage with such a small kitchen?'

'With difficulty!' Bart grinned. 'That will be your problem from now on! And we call it the galley, not kitchen!'

Gill reminded herself mentally to try

to learn the nautical words for things aboard the catamaran! Bart didn't seem put out by her slip, as he continued.

'Pray for unbroken sunshine then we can barbecue on deck.'

'How many passengers do you carry?'

'Usually about ten or twelve. Sometimes we barbecue on the beach somewhere. It depends on what the passengers prefer, and the weather. A sudden squall can play havoc with the best of arrangements but we usually have good warning of storms and can take evasive action. Most of the passengers are pleased to fit in with whatever we suggest, and those who don't get over-ruled by the others! What's your diplomacy like?'

Gill laughed.

'So-so. I've been teaching in a high school for the past three years so I'm used to dealing with awkward characters.'

'A schoolma'am, eh? What subjects?'

'Maths and geography.'

'Could be useful. It should help you with the maps and charts.'

He put his hand under her elbow and steered her towards a narrow doorway opposite the cabin entrance.

'Before we get round to the maps, let me show you your quarters.'

He ushered her through the narrow doorway and turned her to the right. An even narrower door folded back to reveal a small cabin with two bunk beds tucked in neatly to the right and closed lockers on the opposite wall under a shallow rectangular window. A peep through the window revealed that it overlooked the bows. It was small, but had all the bare essentials.

'And where do you and Wak sleep?' she asked curiously, wondering if she had missed a cabin somewhere.

'We'll be sleeping on the seats in the main cabin. They can convert into a double bed but we'll sleep on them as they are. Wak's used to it, and I've done it before. It's not too bad! When you're tired, you'll sleep anywhere!'

'Oh! Have I taken your cabin then?'

'It's no big deal. It's the only way to give you a bit of privacy. It's small in here, but compact. Just these two lockers are free for you to use,' he told her, indicating the ones he meant. 'Various pieces of equipment, spares and such are in the others, but that shouldn't be a problem for you. You seem to travel quite light! Think you can take it? I run a tight ship.'

'I'm no push-over, but I can take it if I deserve it.'

'And if you don't? I'm the captain, and my word goes!'

He took the sting out his words by grinning and Gill made a mock salute.

'Aye, aye, cap'n! Shiver me timbers!'

Bart laughed and backed out of the cabin, gesturing his hand towards the opposite door.

'And there's the heads.'

'Heads?'

'Wash-room and toilet. Read the instructions how to use it. Fresh water is at a premium whilst at sea, and we have to pump every litre on board in port. Since you've elected to be our cleaner, this area is one of your responsibilities.'

Gill peered past him into the compact wash-room. She had no qualms about keeping it clean. A spotless toilet was one of her own particularities.

'That's fine!' she said lightly. 'You've got the necessary equipment?'

'All in the lockers down there. You'll have time to familiarise yourself with it later. OK so far?'

Without waiting for an answer, he steered her back towards the main cabin.

'Anything else you want to know, ask as the occasion arises. I'll just pop up on deck to make sure we're on course. Be looking at the maps and I'll be back with you in a moment.'

Gill scanned the maps on the table, especially the one of the whole island. Glad of her morning tour, which had given her a good over-view of the island, she could see at a glance that Kuah, in the southeast, was the only built-up area of any size and that there was a string of holiday villages in the south west. The international airport was to the north of the holiday villages, with more holiday villages to the northwest of that. The centre of Langkawi seemed to be covered by hills and jungle, and there, in the top north-west corner was their present destination, Datai Bay. Farther round to the north-east were the mangrove swamps and more tiny off-shore islands.

She felt a surge of anticipation. This was going to work out fine!

It was early evening when they dropped anchor in Datai Bay. Dusk had already settled and only the golden glow of electric lighting intermittently sweeping round the curve of the bay revealed the two hotels.

Bart was now dressed in casual blue trousers and a short-sleeved white cotton shirt. Gill was disappointed when he lowered the motorised dinghy and announced that he was going ashore alone.

'You need to stow away your gear, familiarise yourself with the arrangements within the galley and the rest of the boat and look over the menu for tomorrow's buffet lunch,' Bart reminded her. 'I've made arrangements with my suppliers that they will deliver all foodstuff to the Andaman Hotel whilst we are based here, so I'll be confirming my order for tomorrow whilst ashore. Any changes to the menu that you might want to suggest will have to take effect on future occasions, if I agree to them.'

He softened his words with a grin and Gill responded half-heartedly. His decision was sound but she felt like Cinderella being denied the opportunity to go to the ball.

'What about my meal?' she demanded, not wanting to give in too easily. 'I'm hungry.'

'So is Wak. See what's in stock and make something for the two of you. It'll give you practice with our equipment.

You are a crew member, don't forget. It's not for a glorified holiday that I've taken you on!'

'Huh! Slave-driver!' Gill snorted impetuously.

'Too right!' Bart retorted. 'I believe in starting as I mean to go on. If you don't like it, you can always jump ship and swim ashore, but I must remind you that it's a private beach and you won't be welcomed with open arms.'

His eyes threw her a challenge and it was Gill who looked away first. She was taken by the idea of cruising around the island for a few weeks, even as a working cruise, and she didn't want to give up before she had started.

'I'll see you later, then,' she said with a careless shrug of her shoulders. 'Don't do anything I wouldn't do!'

'I'll do my best not to.'

He shimmied down the short ladder with practised ease and stepped into the dinghy. The engine started with the first pull of the cord and he turned to cast off the anchor rope. Gill partly regretted that she was still leaning over the rail watching him when he glanced back up at her but it was too late to step away and pretend that she wasn't, so she smiled and waved a casual goodbye. Bart returned her smile.

'Don't worry. You'll get to know how the other half lives before too long!' he called in parting, and, with that, Gill had to be content.

Leaving the storing of her gear until later, she went into the small galley and rifled through the store cupboard.

'Will an omelette be all right, Wak?' she called out to him eventually, sticking her head through the doorway.

'Yes, miss.'

'Good.'

It was all she could think of and it didn't take long to prepare. They ate it seated on deck in companionable accord, Gill making an occasional question or remark about general matters. Later, she made a swift survey of all the cupboards in the galley and then glanced at the menu for the buffet lunch. It seemed fairly straightforward. There was a selection of barbecued meats and fish, various rice dishes, local vegetables, salads and sauces, and lots of fruit. She felt sure she would be able to manage.

She asked Wak for a general tour around the rest of the boat, especially learning where to find emergency equipment and how to use it. By that time, it was nearly ten o'clock and she went to her tiny cabin to put the contents of her backpack into whatever locker space she could find. She decided to sleep on the lower bunk and use the upper one for storage.

Storing her gear didn't take long. She hoped she wasn't expected to dress up for any functions. Her choice of clothing was severely limited.

Bart hadn't returned when she finally decided to turn in for the night and, although she was sceptical of sleeping soundly in her confined quarters, the gentle rocking of the boat quickly lulled her into a dreamless sleep.

Bart had steered the small dinghy into the shallow waters beyond the coral reef that arced around most of the bay. There was no danger of scraping the keel of the coral, even at low tide, although he wouldn't like to make the same assumption at low tide with the catamaran.

There was no jetty and, as soon as he sensed that the keel was only just skimming the sandy bottom of the sea-bed, he switched off the engine and tipped up the outboard motor, allowing the boat to drift with its own momentum towards the beach. With a practised eye, he judged when to slide over the side into the shallow water, with the mooring rope in his hand, and towed the small craft ashore. It was a lightweight craft and he had no difficulty in drawing it up the beach to above the tide-line.

Even though the sky was now dark, the almost-white sand was clearly visible and it felt soft to his bare feet. He partly regretted not bringing Gill with him. He knew she would have enjoyed it but he had no way of knowing how well she would fit in with his schedule and way of working, and it wouldn't be wise to get himself tied up in something that might not work out.

It probably wouldn't be wise to get too involved anyway. It could cause unnecessary problems. Oh, he liked her and wanted her to fit in. He knew from his island-hopping cruises last year that it was helpful to have a female crew member but he hadn't had a live-on-board female crew member before. It might cause more problems than it solved, and he had enough to contend with, without that, or any other complication.

He didn't want her to be too tired for her first day at work with him. Too much depended on the success of this venture to risk any unnecessary upsets. He reached into the boat for his sandals and strode up the beach with them in his hand, to where he could see the lights from the Beach Bar. He knew the hotel security staff would already be aware of his presence and he lost no time in identifying himself to them, showing them his pass-card.

He then rinsed the sand off his feet at one of the huge water jars placed around the edge of the pool area for that purpose and wriggled his feet into his sandals. He glanced at his watch and was satisfied to see that he had plenty of time for a glass of beer and a small snack so he seated himself by the poolside, enjoying the quiet serenity of the place.

A short while later, refreshed by the beer and food, he stood up and stretched his lithe body. He had business to deal with. The first place he made for was the huge reception area, where he was due to meet the duty manager. The area was spacious and a few guests were seated in various places, enjoying a quiet pre-dinner drink.

He checked with the duty manager how many guests had shown an interest in the cruise trips and was pleased to learn that eight guests had made firm reservations with another two possibles. Well-satisfied, he went down to the kitchen area to discuss the availability of the items on his shopping list with the chef and to finalise his order with his supplier. He had timed his visit to be before the evening meals were being served. Even so, the kitchen was a hive of activity.

'Good evening, Sangkran,' he greeted the chef, a tall Indian Malay, who ran his kitchen with a good-natured efficiency.

'Ah, good evening, Bart,' Sangkran beamed back. 'You are all set to go, are you?'

'That's right. There are eight or ten guests signed up for tomorrow. That's a good number to start with. What did you think of my menu? Is there enough variety in it?'

'It is good. You have plenty of vegetables and pasta dishes in case there are vegetarians. It might be a good idea to ask the guests to request vegetarian meals when they sign up, just in case you ever get a whole party of them.'

'Good idea, thanks. I'll do that in future. Is it a good time for me to be using the kitchen phone to ring my supplier?'

Sangkran waved his hand towards it.

'Be my guest. And, now, if you will excuse me, the early diners will be arriving soon.'

Bart returned his cheerful wave and spent the next ten minutes talking to his supplier, arranging for his goods to be delivered early the next morning, the meats and fish ready for cooking, other ingredients ready to serve, with everything packed in two large cool boxes that he would take on board with him in the morning. Pleased with the success of his visit, Bart bade Sangkran, farewell as he left the kitchen and sauntered back through the hotel, out to the poolside. It was still quite early and he decided to have another drink and a more substantial meal.

In the short while since he had left it, the Beach Bar was now crowded, with sounds of numerous male voices and loud laughter ringing out. Someone was having a good time! However, when Bart caught the eye of a waiter, his request for the menu was met with an apology.

'It is a private function, sir,' the young man said with regret, adding by way of explanation, 'It is a conference party.'

'Ah, sorry! I didn't realise. Never mind. Another time, perhaps.'

The appetising aroma was making him feel hungry and he hoped there was something on board that he could knock up into something edible.

'Care to join us?' a voice asked as he turned to leave.

Bart turned in the direction of the voice, to where a few men of about his own age were standing by the bar, drinks in hand.

'I'm not a guest here,' Bart explained

and waved vaguely towards the beach. 'I'm just passing by.'

'There's enough food for one more. We're a conference group and I bet everyone won't turn up. It's the last night and I heard of one or two who needed to make a quick departure. Hey, Joni, he's with us, OK?'

The waiter waved a hand in acknowledgement and Bart thanked the man. The man raised his glass.

'What're you having?'

'A beer, please, but allow me.'

'No need. It's all laid on for us.'

'Oh, right! Thanks, then.'

He gestured towards the main part of the hotel.

'Not a bad place to come for a conference, is it?'

'Too right!' The man laughed.

The evening passed quickly and Bart found himself accepted into the group, enjoying the casual conversations and male company as they ate the lavish buffet and flow of drinks. It was with regret that he eventually took his leave of them. He felt pleasantly replenished and although he knew he had had a bit more to drink than he normally had, he was by no means too drunk to be in sole charge of the dinghy.

He headed towards the beach. There was no path at this point but the ground felt firm beneath his feet. As he emerged from the trees on to the softer texture of the sand, he began to bend down to take off his sandals, preferring to walk barefooted on the sand.

The downward movement brought a flood of bright lights flashing across his eyes, making him feel as though he was about to lose his balance. Unnerved by the sensation, he tried to straighten his posture. As he did so, he was vaguely aware of a swift movement beside him, but before he could turn, something struck him on the side of his head and he pitched forward into an all-enveloping blackness.

3

Gill awoke to the gentle rocking of the boat and lay still for a moment as memories of the previous day came flooding back into her consciousness. Daylight had already broken and when she raised herself on to her elbows to look out of the small window overlooking the bows, she could see the brilliant blue sky.

Feeling a rush of adrenalin, she quickly scrambled out of the narrow bunk, grabbed hold of her toilet bag and towel and darted out of the cabin, across the gangway and into the washroom, thankfully meeting neither of her male companions. The sight of the blue sea had given her the urge for an early-morning swim. Her ablutions completed, she darted back to her cabin and swiftly pulled on her bikini.

When she emerged on to the deck,

she was immediately aware that something was wrong. There was no sight of Bart, and Wak was staring shoreward with a perplexed expression on his face.

'What's the matter, Wak?'

'Mr Bart, he not return to ship last night. It not like him.'

He pointed towards the shore.

'The dinghy is still there. See!'

Gill looked and could see the dinghy resting on the sand between the water and the trees. As they watched, two dark-skinned figures emerged from the trees, ran over to the dinghy and looked inside. Although Gill couldn't hear what was being said, it was clear that something in the boat was causing some perplexity.

'What d'you think's happening?' Gill asked Wak.

'I don't know. See, they pull someone up!'

The two male figures were now supporting another figure in a sitting position and it was obvious from his clothing that it was Bart. Gill could see him putting a hand to his head and then drop his head between his knees.

'It's Bart! Oh, no! He looks ill or something! What can we do, Wak? We need to get to him.'

She looked hesitantly down at the water. She had wanted a swim, but it was a fair distance to shore from where they were anchored.

'Can we sail any nearer, Wak?' she asked.

'It is low tide. The boat might scrape the coral. It do damage. Anyway, no worry! See! They bring Mr Bart and our dinghy!'

It seemed as though Wak was correct. The two figures had now been joined by some more and, after pointing out to sea to the catamaran, two of them pulled another boat out of the boat-house and down the sand to the sea. They then helped Bart to walk out to it and once he was on board, two of them dragged the dinghy across the sand to join the other.

Gill and Wak couldn't see all that was

happening but eventually the two boats were heading across the bay towards them. Gill left Wak to see to tying up their own dinghy and she hovered by the gap in the rail at the stern where two Malaysian lads were helping Bart to climb up the short ladder. He looked as though his legs were about give way under him, even though he was protesting.

'I'm all right now. Thanks, lads. I owe you one.'

'You don't look all right!' Gill pronounced. 'Whatever happened?'

She looked in bewilderment from Bart to the two Malaysians.

'Has he spent the night on the beach?'

'He drink too much, miss!' one of the Malaysians said with a grin, making a drinking gesture with his hand. 'He have big head today!'

'Oh, Bart! How could you?' Gill reproached him. 'Today of all days! What about the cruise?'

'I'm all right, I tell you! Just make me

a cup of black coffee!'

'We go back now,' one of the Malaysians said as Bart lurched into the cabin. 'He sleep it off, yes?'

'Yes, I hope so,' Gill agreed.

She followed Bart into the main cabin where he had collapsed on to one of the side seats, his head in his hands.

'What happened?' she asked sharply.

'I don't know. I can't remember,' he groaned. 'Look, make me that coffee, will you, Gill? That'll clear my head. I feel awful!'

And you deserve it, she thought, as she flounced into the galley, disappointed by the turn of events. She couldn't believe he had been so irresponsible as to get drunk the night before his first cruise from the hotel. It just showed how wrong you could be about a person. She boiled some water and spooned in a generous helping of coffee granules. She then added a drop of cold water so that he would be able to drink it immediately.

'Here!' she said, handing him the

steaming mug and looking at her watch. 'It's nearly seven o'clock. What time do you have to be back at the hotel to collect the food and the guests? I presume there are some guests wanting a cruise, or is that why you got too drunk, to drown your sorrows?'

'What?' He paused from sipping the coffee and looked up at her. 'I'm not drunk! At least . . . '

He closed his eyes and gently shook his head, wincing with the effort. He touched the side of his head and winced again.

'That's sore!'

'Let me see.'

Gill touched his head gently, parting his hair a little.

'It looks a bit swollen. You probably hit it on something. Did you collapse in the dinghy?'

'I don't know. I don't think so! And I'm not drunk! Heavens, girl, I know what being drunk feels like, and I'm not!'

'Then how did you bang your head?'

'I don't know! Maybe I walked into a tree.'

'And you're not drunk? Do you normally walk into trees? Or, maybe the tree walked into you!'

'It was dark! But not that dark! I could see the sea, and I'd reached the sand.'

He paused, trying to recall the end of his evening ashore.

'I felt strange, but I've told you, I wasn't drunk! I think someone hit me!'

'Why would anyone do that?'

'I don't know.'

Gill pursed her lips. She wasn't sure whether she was convinced by his explanation or not. It seemed a bit unlikely. However, the main question was, what now?

'Is there a cruise today or not, and, if there is, do you feel fit enough?'

'Yes, and yes. I have to be!'

'So, what time do you have to be at the hotel?'

'About half past eight, I think. That will give me time to collect the food boxes and ship them out to you and go back to collect the guests.'

'How many are there?'

'Eight definites. It'll be two boat-loads, plus the food run.'

'Which gives you just over an hour to get yourself together. D'you want some breakfast?'

'No, thanks. I had a good meal last night.'

She made some toast, enough for them all, poured some muesli into a bowl for herself and put some pieces of fruit into a dish. In spite of his earlier refusal, Bart helped himself to toast and seemed brighter when he had eaten it.

'What needs doing before the guests arrive?' Gill wanted to know. 'I was going to have a swim but I don't think I've got time now.'

'No. It's best to swim before breakfast. Don't worry, you'll have plenty of chances to swim later. A word of advice — make sure you cover up during the heat of the day. You'll burn easily and the breeze can be deceptive.'

'Are you always this bossy?'

'Only on board ship!' Bart replied with a grin.

He was looking more like himself now and Gill felt herself becoming more hopeful that the day would go well.

'Will shorts and T-shirt be OK?'

'That's fine. You can save your glad rags for when I take you to dinner somewhere.'

'Is that an invitation?'

'It might be! Is that an acceptance?'

'It might be!'

They grinned at each other, then Bart snapped into business mode.

'Right! Let's see how we make out this week, then, shall we?'

He stood up carefully, making sure he was balanced properly before bringing the charts back on to the table.

'I'll show you where we're going today and give you an idea about the timetable. This is where we are now. We're going to sail back down the west side of the island but going inshore of these small islands, meandering along throughout the morning and heading for this larger island here, Pulau Dayang Bunting. Pulau means island, so you'll see the word a lot on the maps and charts.'

'Is it an inhabited island?'

'Only by a few Malays. Visitors are mostly day visitors, like ourselves. The main attraction is the Lake Of The Pregnant Maiden. You'll need to read up about the legend in that yellow book over there. Briefly, a couple who had been trying to have a baby for about twenty years were successful after they drank the water from the lake, so infertile couples make the journey here in hope of the same success. It's a freshwater lake and is good for swimming and boating. We'll let the guests spend an hour or so there while we barbecue the lunch and either set it up on a secluded little beach nearby or in the main cabin.

'Then, depending on what the guests want, they can either stay around there and swim for a while or move on around the coast to here where we can feed the eagles for a while before making our way back round the coast to Datai Bay, dropping them off round about five o'clock, in time to get showered and dressed for dinner. A simple trip but usually very much enjoyed. Any questions?'

'What do I do, besides barbecuing lunch, that is?'

'You act as hostess, handing out drinks, mainly fruit drinks, but I carry cans of beer and lager. It's all in the price so there's no money to be collected. They'll pay at the hotel before we start. You make sure everyone is happy and watch over any children who come aboard. They are their parents' responsibility mainly but it's always good to keep an eye on them. Anything else?'

'Not at the moment. I'll ask if I need to do so.'

'Good. Right, then, let's make sure everywhere is clean and ship-shape and then we can make a start. You do the galley today. I'll have a shower and then do the washroom today and, Wak, you check over the outboard motor, with it having been beached all night, will you? And make sure there's enough fuel in it. We've got forty minutes, so chop-chop!'

Gill was glad Bart had recovered sufficiently to take control and set to cleaning the galley. At twenty past eight, everywhere was bright and clean and they were ready to take the dinghy ashore to collect the stores.

'I'll leave Wak on board today,' Bart decided. 'I want to show you, Gill, where to go to get to the kitchens and, whilst you're seeing to that, I'm going to see if I can identify any of the conference party I was with last night to see if they heard or saw anything that might throw light on who knocked me out. You never know. Someone might have seen something without knowing what it was about.'

Gill dressed in shorts and T-shirt,

eagerly slipped down the short ladder into the dinghy for her first trip ashore. The sea was calm and they motored over the clear water, over the coral reef and into the even calmer water of the inner bay. They pulled the dinghy above the waterline and Bart led the way through the shrubbery to the poolside, where he showed her how to rinse the sand off her feet before proceeding any farther.

He led the way round the back of the hotel to the kitchen, where Gill looked around with interest as they threaded their way through to the chef's office. Sangkran rose from his chair to greet them.

'Good morning, my friend. You are well? I am happy to see you, and your companion. No sore head, eh?'

Bart ignored the final remark and drew Gill forward to introduce her.

'This is Gill Madison, one of my crew. She may come on her own to collect the food order some days. Gill, this is Sangkran, the head chef.

Anything he doesn't know about the preparation of food isn't worth knowing!'

They shook hands cordially, as Bart continued, 'And I'm perfectly well, thank you, Sangkran. What makes you ask so specifically?'

'It was mentioned that you had over-enjoyed yourself last night. How do you say it? A small bird told me? We have many small birds here!'

'Word travels fast, especially the wrong word! I wasn't drunk, Sangkran. See, this is what made me pass out.'

He leaned forward and parted his hair slightly. Sangkran peered at it.

'Hmm. There is a slight swelling. Does it still hurt?'

'A little.'

'I will make a small compress for you. It is a hobby of mine. I learn about old herbal remedies and mix them myself. But it is a strange place to bang your head by falling over. How did it happen?'

'I didn't fall. I was hit!'

Bart told him all he knew and Sangkran looked quite perturbed.

'But who would do this to you? We do not have problems here like in the cities. Were you robbed?'

'No, nothing. I haven't a clue who did it, nor why, but I'd like to find out. Look, Sangkran, may I leave Gill with you to check the order and see to getting it to the boat? I want to go to the restaurant to see if I can recognise anyone from the conference party I was invited to join last evening. Someone among them might have seen something.'

'I think you have missed them, Bart. They had an early breakfast and early pick-up for the airport. But go, anyway. We will manage everything here, won't we, Miss Madison?'

'Call me Gill, please, and, yes, we'll manage fine. I'll be asking you for some tips on how to cook all this. That is, if you'll let me in on any of your trade secrets!'

She had taken an instant liking to

him. He was so friendly and open and, with Bart now departed, he willingly gave her hints on how long to expect the various meats and fish to take to cook and gave her a few small, sealed dishes of sauces to serve with the various items. When everything had been checked, he told her to sit in his office whilst he made up the compress for Bart's bruise. He returned after some five minutes or so with a small pot of a creamy-looking mixture.

'Put this on a cool cloth and place it on the swelling as soon as you get back to the boat. Tell Bart to lie quietly for half an hour and the soreness should disappear. Keep it in your refrigerator and repeat it tonight if there is still any sign of the swelling. Throw it away after that, as it needs to be used fresh.'

'What's in it exactly?'

'Aha, that is my secret.' Sangkran smiled. 'But, just for you, I tell you the main ingredients are rosemary, lavender and fresh milk, mixed to my own special recipe. You tell me how well it works, as I like to keep a record of each case. As I said, it is my hobby and I like to think I am doing good to humanity.'

Gill took the pot off him and he called over some of his kitchen porters and told them to carry the cool-boxes along to the dinghy for her. Gill went with them and was joined by Bart as the boxes were being loaded. On the way back to the catamaran, she told him about the compress Sangkran had made for him.

'Well, it will have to wait until later,' Bart objected. 'I've got to go back to the hotel to meet our guests in less than half an hour. Only six, I'm afraid. The others seem to have heard a tale that we weren't sailing today and have chosen to do something else. Not that it matters. The fewer the better today, the way I'm feeling!'

'Couldn't I collect the guests?' Gill asked.

'I didn't take you to Reception. You won't know where to go.'

'I've got a tongue in my head, haven't

I? I'll put on my best schoolma'am voice and I'll have them eating out of my hand!'

'I bet you will and all!' Bart grinned.

'Right! That's settled,' Gill pronounced firmly.

In their absence, Wak had been busy swilling down the deck and making everywhere look bright and shiny. Gill persuaded Bart to let her apply the compress straight away and suggested he lie down in her cabin since that was the only place he would get any peace whilst she unpacked the boxes and stored everything where she would know where to find it later.

The next half-hour flew by and Gill had only just stored everything away when it was time to get Wak to take her ashore. Bart assured her that he was feeling a lot brighter and could hardly feel the tenderness on his head.

'So, I'm back on watch, and don't you forget it!' he said with a grin.

'Aye, aye, cap'n!'

Gill grinned back, making her mock

salute. She waved papers at him.

'I'll hand out these fliers advertising the cruises to any guests I see, shall I? It won't do any harm to remind people we're up and running, will it?'

Bart agreed and Gill happily made the return trip across the bay. She had a clipboard ready with the names of the expected guests to be ticked off as they registered and paid for their day out. Leaving Wak in charge of the dinghy, she followed Bart's directions to Reception, handing out the leaflets as she went. A group of four young men at the poolside assured her they'd book for tomorrow's trip straightaway if she were on board.

'Too right I am!' She laughed. 'See you tomorrow!'

As she neared the Reception, a casually-dressed man of medium height, in his mid-twenties she guessed, called her back, as he frowned at the leaflet in his hand.

'What's all this to you?' he asked bluntly in a clear English accent.

'I'm part of the crew.'

'Since when?'

His eyes, as he regarded her closely, were somewhat cold and Gill involuntarily shivered, in spite of the heat.

'Since yesterday,' she said somewhat defensively.

The man hesitated and it seemed to Gill that he had spoken without thinking. Unexpectedly, he laughed.

'You're not what I would expect of a low-paid crew member. Skippers usually get the cheapest crew to make more profit. Girlfriend, are you?'

'No, not that it's any of your business.'

'How did you get the job?'

'What's that to you?'

'Just curious. I . . . er . . . know someone who would like to crew for a season. I thought I could tell her how to go about it.'

Gill was instantly wary. Who was this fellow? What did he know? She had the uncomfortable feeling that he knew she hadn't got the job legitimately. But why should it have anything to do with him — unless he knew Bart. She had better be careful what she said.

'Tell her to go to an agency,' she suggested nonchalantly over her shoulder. 'That's the usual way.'

'Is that how you did it?'

Gill pretended she hadn't heard, and waved a casual hand towards him.

'See you around!' she said airily. 'Maybe book a cruise, eh?'

But she hoped he wouldn't. She couldn't shake off the idea that he had expected someone else to be on Bart's crew and, if he knew Bart, he might expose her for the opportunist that she was.

She found the reception area and glanced around. It was beautiful. In spite of there being guests making enquiries at the desk, it was a calm, restful place. Smiling, Gill walked over to the desk, where a family group and a middle-aged couple looked as though they were waiting for someone.

'Hello! Mr and Mrs Whitcombe and

Mr and Mrs Cookson? I'm Gill Madison of Sunshine Cruises. Are you our guests for the day?'

The older woman looked relieved.

'Yes, we are. We weren't sure . . . that is, we'd heard rumours . . . '

'That we weren't operating today? Completely unfounded, I assure you.' She smiled at the children. 'Hi, you two! Got your sea-legs ready?'

'I have. My name's Rebecca. I'm seven and I'm a good sailor! Mark's only four! He's going to be sea-sick!'

'No, I'm not! I'm just as good a sailor as you are!' the little boy asserted.

'I hope you are, Mark. You look as though you will be!'

Gill turned back to the adults.

'If you'll excuse me a moment, I must speak to the receptionist. You've got your swim towels and plenty of sun lotion? Good. I won't be a minute.'

She crossed over to the duty desk and introduced herself, showing Bart's security card, and asked if there were any special instructions she should know. After a brief chat, she returned to the small group, checked their names against her register, took their payment and asked them to accompany her down to the beach.

As they left the reception area, she had the uncomfortable feeling that she was being watched and, when she glanced over her shoulder, she caught a brief glimpse of the man she had talked to earlier. He was standing with another man and pointing in her direction. As she paused and looked at them, they drew back and leaned over the balustrade of the open balcony that overlooked the swimming pool and continued in conversation. She turned away, wondering if she had mistaken their interest in her, but she had the uncomfortable feeling that she hadn't.

The other man was dressed in a dark business suit. He was tall, slender with short black hair and a tanned complexion. He looked about thirty, she thought. When she glanced over her shoulder again, he had drawn back into the shade of a tall pot plant but she knew he was still watching her, and that she was being discussed.

Well, they would know her again, she decided — and had the disturbing premonition that they meant trouble.

4

Whilst Wak was tying up the dinghy, Gill led the six guests to the deck area at the bows, pointing out that they could either settle on the main deck or slide on to the rigid netting that was fixed between the two keels of the catamaran.

'Wow! That's great!' Rebecca whooped.

'Life-jackets for the children!' Gill insisted. 'Adults, too, if there are any non-swimmers.'

'We can swim!' the two children chimed together.

'Good, and I bet you're great!' Gill smiled. 'You can show me later, when we've anchored somewhere safe, but you still need to wear life-jackets while we're sailing. Did you see the name of the catamaran?'

'Yes. Pega . . . Pega-something.'

'Pegasus,' Gill supplied. 'A flying

horse, in Greek mythology, and we'll be flying over waves once we get going. You'll be safe on the netting but I don't want to risk losing you overboard, not before you've had the delicious barbecue lunch, anyway! So, come on, let's try you for size.'

Once she had them safely kitted out, they crawled on to the netting, watching the sea slip away beneath them.

'Now, drinks for everyone!' she invited. 'We have plenty of fruit juices, beers and lagers and other specialities. Here's the list.'

The two children were enthralled by everything and the older couple, Anne and Harry, became surrogate grandparents for the day, giving Sarah and Peter, the children's parents, some leisure time to relax in the sun. When everyone was settled, Bart beckoned Gill to follow him to the stern.

'Come and see this,' he invited with a grin.

Glancing down between the rear

sections of the twin hulls, Gill could see a large dragnet attached to a low rear platform and suspended in the water between the two hulls. It looked like a trawler net.

'Are you hoping to catch some fish?' she asked.

'No. It's our high-speed, deluxe Jacuzzi. D'you want to try it?'

Gill raised an eyebrow. Was he teasing her?

'Now?'

'Why not? Everyone's happy back there and Wak will keep an eye on them for a few minutes. You need to try it, then you can help with it. Come on. Slip out of your shorts. You'll enjoy it.'

Gill hesitated only for a second or two. He wouldn't be teasing her, not with guests on board. Even so, she felt slightly apprehensive.

'Just hold on here with your left hand,' Bart instructed her, taking her hand in his and placing it on a low rail. 'Now, just roll over backwards to your right and let go.'

She could feel his breath on her skin and was aware of the strangest sensations coursing through her body. Her heart felt as though it might stop beating and she couldn't prevent a small gasp escaping from her lips.

She was acutely aware that the effect his closeness was having on her senses was more unsettling than her reluctance to tumble herself off the stability of the deck into the frothing water below.

'OK, I'm going!'

Before she could change her mind, she tossed herself backwards. The roughness of the net was around her body before she had time to wonder if she had indeed missed the net. For a frantic second or so, she gripped the tough netting at each side of her and scrabbled her heels to secure a foothold, but she realised quickly that she was held securely within the confines of the net. As she relaxed, the water frothed and bubbled around her, invigorating her skin. She looked up into Bart's laughing eyes.

'It's great!' she whooped. 'Come and join me!'

'I wish I could,' and he did indeed look as regretful as he sounded. 'I'll have to postpone that pleasure to a later time, when we have no guests to keep watch over. As will you, I'm sorry to say, now that you're in! Stay for a few more minutes whilst I bring the guests along to show them, then you can give them a demonstration of how to get in it. It will hold the four adults and both children, if they all want to go in it together but I'll need you to be on life-guard duty, just in case!'

Gill lay back in the net and enjoyed the sensation whilst she was able, knowing there would be many other opportunities, reminding herself that this was work! Scrambling out of the net, under the watchful gaze of the guests, was actually more difficult than tumbling in, and rather more undignified! Gill was glad of the helping hand that Bert extended towards her.

She slid gracefully out of his arms

and slicked back her hair as she resumed the position from where she had back-flipped into the net.

'It's easy, folks!' She grinned at her audience. 'See, left hand here, and back-flip in! Wheee!'

Shaking the water out of her eyes as she lay back in the net.

'Who's for joining me? Anne?'

With some encouragement, Anne was soon beside her and Gill scrambled out to make way for the other guests. Only Mark needed to be handed down into his mother's arms and, for the next twenty minutes or so, the whole party was happily entertained in the dragnet Jacuzzi.

Bart took advantage of the opportunity to teach Gill some rudiments of sailing, until her head was buzzing with terms like spinnaker, mainsail, jib, tack, halyard, winches, shrouds and stanchions.

'I'll never remember all those!' she groaned. 'Let alone what to do!'

'You will,' Bart assured her. 'It's not

much different from sailing smaller crafts. There's just more of everything!'

'I suppose so,' Gill agreed ruefully. 'You and Wak make it look so easy.'

'Practice makes perfect, my girl!' Bart grinned at her. 'I'll run through it once more then you can go and tell your guests that we'll soon be sailing among the small islands around the south-west coast of Langkawi. They usually like to be on deck for that.'

Sure enough, all four adults elected to return to the deck, promising Rebecca and Mark that there would be more opportunities to be in the dragnet later. Bart gave an entertaining running commentary as they weaved their way among the small islands and then they headed eastward to Palua Dayang Bunting and their port of call for the next two hours.

Bart lowered the anchor offshore and designated Wak to run their guests ashore to visit the freshwater Lake of the Pregnant Maiden after Gill had recounted the legend to them.

'You can either hire small boats on the lake, paddle-boats and rowing boats or hire a speedboat-towed banana boat, or you can just swim in the fresh water,' Gill advised.

Gill and Bart watched on board as Wak steered the small motorboat round the headland and out of sight.

'We'll do the barbecue whilst they're away,' Bart told Gill. 'But, first, a much-needed swim! Come on! Race you!'

He dragged off his shirt and stepped out of his shorts as he spoke and made a graceful dive over the side of the boat, entering the deep water with hardly a splash. Gill was only seconds after him. The water was crystal clear and Gill could see Bart's tanned legs rising to the surface ahead of her. Not wanting to appear too eager for close contact, she twisted around and surfaced farther away. She lay back in the water and flipped her legs, moving farther away. It was heavenly!

They swam separately for a while. Bart struck out for the nearby shore using a fast crawl that Gill knew she had no hope of emulating. Instead, she chose to swim around the yacht and through the slightly eerie atmosphere between the two hulls, where the water seemed to change to a translucent green. She made a few surface dives into the clear water, catching an elusive glimpse of some brightly-coloured fish.

Eventually she saw Bart swimming back and sculled idly on her back as he drew nearer.

'Race you twice around the boat!' he called when he was still a few metres away. 'That way. I'll give you a start.'

Gill didn't demur. She knew she would need the advantage. She flipped her body over and struck out in the direction he had indicated. It wasn't long before Bart had overtaken her. Before she had made one circuit, he had passed her again but, when she had completed her two circuits, he was nowhere to be seen.

Gill trod water, wondering if he had returned aboard but he suddenly emerged beside her.

'Got you!' he called out, putting his hands on her shoulders.

His laughing eyes seemed to soften as he looked at her and a slight forward movement of his head made Gill sure he was going to kiss her. In evasive action, she took a deep breath of air and stiffened her body, sinking beneath the water. She knew Bart had followed her and opened her eyes to see exactly where he was. His face was level with her, his hair seeming to stand up on end as he sank beneath it. She grinned at him, knowing her hair would be looking the same.

Bart touched her shoulders once more, gently, this time, and he jerked his head upwards slightly. With a flick of her feet, Gill obeyed, not resisting when she felt Bart pull her closer, nor when he placed his mouth carefully over hers in a gentle kiss. It felt erotic, arousing her senses in a way she had never experienced before. The intensity of her feelings shocked her. She wasn't sure she wanted this, pleasant though it was!

Before she could analyse the depth of her reaction, their heads had broken the surface and, feeling short of breath, Gill automatically pulled her head away, frantically treading water whilst she regained her breath and, hopefully, her composure. Bart was grinning delightedly. For some unaccountable reason, it infuriated her.

'Some kiss!' he marvelled.

Huh! That wasn't the first time he had kissed a girl underwater!

'Like a jelly fish!' she spat at him, twisting away and swimming towards the steps at the stern of the boat.

'An electric eel, more like!' Bart rejoined, as he struck out behind her.

Gill hauled herself out of the water and stood at the top of the steps, looking down at him as he prepared to follow her up the steps. She wanted to say something cutting to him but couldn't think what to say. The seawater was glistening on his tanned body as he pulled himself out of the water and the sight of his fine physique reminded her how much she had enjoyed his kiss. Unconsciously, her fingers touched her lips and the tingling sensation she felt there quelled her annoyance.

She turned away abruptly, saying over her shoulder, 'You had better show me how to start the barbecue,' hoping that Bart was unaware of the effect his kiss had had on her. Did she really want this? She needed time to think about it.

To her relief, Bart made no further move on her. He concentrated on getting the barbecue grill out of the locker where it was stored under some of the seats. Working in harmony, they soon had it assembled and Bart lifted the heavy gas cylinder out of another locker.

'I don't expect you to do this on your own. It's too heavy,' he explained. 'Unless the weather is bad, there'll always be at least two of us to do the cooking. We'll start with the chicken legs and the fish. The chilli-fried beef is part-cooked and the tiger prawns won't take long. Once we've got it laid out on the grill, I'll keep an eye on it whilst you put a cloth on the table and lay out the cold vegetable dishes and the salads.'

Gill agreed and five minutes later she had cleared the table and was arranging a delicious array of food spread on it. It looked very tempting and made her aware of how hungry she was feeling.

Echoing her thoughts, Bart called through the doorway.

'Put enough plates out for us as well. We'll eat with the guests since there are so few of them, and put a selection of everything straight into the fridge for later. There's plenty of food with us having the two cancellations. Oh, and put some clothes on before you come back on deck!'

Gill bristled. How dare he! Was he implying she was flaunting herself? He hadn't objected earlier! And he was still wearing his swimming shorts.

'I'll decide when I need to cover myself!' she retorted indignantly, furiously aware that a warm flush was spreading over her features.

Bart grinned disarmingly at her.

'I'm not criticising you,' he said mildly. 'You look great. I'm just cautioning you on the amount of exposure to the sun you've had. I don't want you to end up with sunburn. It can be pretty painful and it's now the hottest part of the day.'

Gill felt a bit foolish. She shouldn't have jumped down his throat like that! He was right, she needed to be careful.

'Sorry,' she muttered ungraciously. 'I thought . . . '

Bart nodded, dismissing her apology.

'Just looking after my crew!'

He gave an airy wave and disappeared, leaving Gill to recover her poise. She knew she had been ultra-sensitive towards him. It was because of the way her body reacted to his close presence. Maybe she shouldn't be quite so reluctant to flirt a bit with him. What harm could there be? Holiday romances happened all the time, without the world coming to an end when they fizzled out. Only, somehow, she sensed she would feel more deeply about him than that, if ever she let herself, that was! Then, the time would come when she had to leave to return to England and Bart would stay here, where his hopes and dreams for his own yachting business were centred.

No, it was best to remain aloof, friendly but detached. Thus decided, she went up on deck to retrieve her shorts and T-shirt from where she had abandoned them, managing to behave quite naturally towards Bart as she slipped them back on again.

'How's it going?' she called over to him.

'Fine. Another twenty minutes or so and it will be ready.'

He nodded towards the headland.

'There'll be time for the guests to have a swim before lunch if they wish.'

She followed his glance and could see

that Wak was on his way back with the guests. The hour had flown by, as did the next, as the guests took the opportunity to swim and splash around the boat for a while, until they were summoned back on board to eat their lunch. It was a happy, relaxed occasion and they were fully appreciative of the lavish spread that had been prepared for them.

'When you're all ready to move on, we'll cruise around Pulau Tuba, the adjacent island,' Bart announced eventually, 'and then we'll call in at Kuah for an hour or so. There is a landscaped folklore theme park next to the jetty where the children might like to go and a variety of shops for you to visit.'

Amidst murmurs of approval, Gill began to clear away the remnants of the lunch, putting the plates of excess fruit into the refrigerator to be handed round later, leaving the guests to either sample the Jacuzzi again or sunbathe on the deck.

As they approached Kuah, Bart

reminded Gill to help Wak get out the fenders to hang over the sides to protect the boat from banging into the jetty. She felt quite professional as she copied Wak's action and then stood ready to leap ashore with a mooring line in her hand as Bart skilfully brought the catamaran alongside the jetty.

Wak tied up his end and then came to show Gill how to loop the rope around the capstan. She wondered if she would soon be able to do it with such a quick, fluid movement. Bart had lowered a gangplank for the guests.

'Be back here in one hour's time,,' he reminded them.

'What are we going to do?' Gill asked.

'I need to replenish our store of soft drinks,' Bart replied. 'I haven't room to store as much as I would like to on board and they are cheaper from here than if I get them from the supplier at the hotel. Wak can come to help me carry them, if you don't mind staying on board on your own. Is there anything you need?'

'I could do with some more sun cream, factor twelve,' Gill remembered. 'Apart from that, I'm OK.'

'Right! You're in charge.'

He grinned and made a mock salute and Gill watched as he and Wak strolled along the jetty towards the town.

She busied herself tidying the cabin and making sure the washroom was clean. Satisfied that everything was in order, she went back on deck to take advantage of the sunshine before the daily mid-afternoon shower of heavy rain descended on them. A young woman of about her own age was standing on the jetty, staring at the boat. She was dressed in casual jeans and a white close-fitting top with a plunging neckline. In one hand was a tattered holdall. Her dark hair was tied back with a yellow scarf and a petulant frown marred her otherwise pretty face.

'Can I help you?' Gill enquired.

'Where's the owner?' the girl demanded. 'Bart Lawson, I believe.'

'He's gone ashore,' Gill told her. 'He won't be long. Is there anything I can do for you?'

'Too right there is!' the girl said smartly. 'You can get off that boat and high-tail it out of here! That's my job you've taken, and I want it back!'

5

Gill stared at the girl, realising this must be the girl sent by the agency, but was she really justified in claiming the job now? Bart had needed her yesterday but she hadn't turned up. Surely, she had lost it by default.

She realised suddenly how much she wanted to keep the job. She was enjoying it and, in spite of her doubts about the wisdom of being attracted to Bart, she knew the attraction was there, mutually she felt, and she wanted to get to know him better.

'I'm sorry, but you're too late,' she told the girl. 'When you didn't turn up, Bart hired me instead.'

'Then he'll just have to un-hire you, won't he?' the girl snapped. 'The job's mine by right.'

She patted a rear pocket of her jeans. 'I've got the letter from the agency to prove it. So, you may as well shove off now and save embarrassment all round.'

Gill felt her hackles rise. Maybe the girl did have a letter from the agency, but she had still missed the boat by twenty-four hours. Possession was nine-tenths of the law, after all! She moved to stand at the top of she short gangway and folded her arms decisively.

'I'm not going anywhere!' Gill declared. 'So it's up to you to leave, or stay right there until Bart returns.'

She glared at the girl, instinctively disliking her. It seemed as though the antipathy was mutual, as the girl glared back, pure malice in her eyes.

'I've got right on my side. You stole my job. I'll get Bart banned by the tourist trade if he doesn't stick by this agreement.'

Gill felt a flurry of alarm. She didn't want Bart's business to suffer on her behalf, but, still, the girl hadn't turned up on time. Surely that broke the agreement. Even so, she had the niggling misapprehension that she had misled Bart into thinking that she had come from the agency. Too late, she now regretted that. She was certain Bart would have still hired her, if only out of desperation. What if he now felt she had unfairly duped him?

Looking along the jetty, she knew that time was running out for one of them. Bart and Wak were returning, thankfully before the passengers. They were both carrying a few large packs of canned drinks, their chins resting on the top layer. Gill deliberately didn't look towards them so that the dark-haired girl wouldn't have the advantage of rushing up to Bart before he was within earshot of the boat. There was no way she wished to lose her dignity by having the two of them racing up to him like two naughty schoolgirls, each wanting to get in their side of the tale first. Even so, the outcome wasn't much better.

Bart sensed something was amiss by the stances the two girls had adopted, like two hunters stalking the same prey, neither willing to step aside or walk away.

'Anything wrong, Gill?' he asked when he was near enough to speak.

'It appears so,' Gill began, her face showing signs of tension. 'This girl . . . '

The girl turned to face Bart, all rancour disappearing from her demeanour as an appealing smile lit her features.

'Are you Bart Lawson?' she enquired pleasantly, thrusting out her hand. 'My name's Tiffany Browne, with an 'e',' she added, smiling winsomely.

Bart placed his right foot on the nearby capstan and rested the weight of the trays of cans on his knee, freeing his right hand to shake Tiffany's awkwardly.

'Hi, Tiffany Browne-with-an-e,' he returned her greeting. 'And how may I help you?'

'I was just thanking my temporary stand-in for her co-operation.' She smiled up at him, her long, dark lashes framing her dark brown eyes. 'I'm sorry for the delay in my arrival but I'm sure the agency told Miss Whatever-her-name-is the score when they sent her along and she will have explained it to you.'

'Er, no, I don't think she did,' Bart said, swinging his gaze towards Gill. 'Was there a message, Gill?'

Gill could feel the blood rushing up her neck and over her face.

'No, there wasn't,' she said shortly. 'I didn't come from an agency. I just happened to be here when you desperately needed another crew member. You took me on face value, as I took you. We shook hands on it, remember?'

Bart nodded.

'Yes, I do remember,' he agreed.

He eyed Gill questioningly but she decided to fight her corner with the same blatant composure as Tiffany. She smiled disarmingly.

'You needed another member of crew, I needed a job, which I still do.'

'So do I!' Tiffany snapped, momentarily forgetting her demure rôle.

She recovered her poise quickly and

moved closer to Bart, swaying her narrow hips.

'Look, I'll level with you, Bart. I've no money and I've nowhere to go. I really do need this job. I'm counting on it, in fact. I've got loads of experience.'

I bet you have, Gill thought sourly.

'With boats?' Bart asked, his interest caught.

'Of course! What else could I mean?' Tiffany asked with wide-eyed innocence, her eyelashes fluttering.

Bart grinned, exchanging a brief almost conspiratorial glance with Tiffany that wasn't lost on Gill. Her eyes narrowed as she awaited his response. Couldn't he see that Tiffany had him on a line and was reeling him in?

'I can't afford three crew members,' he said flatly. 'Wak is permanent, so it's between you two girls. I'm sorry, Gill was here and you weren't, Tiffany.'

'But the agency . . . '

'It's only an introduction, not an agreement. I'm at liberty to hire or not hire whomever I wish. Sorry, Tiffany.

Another time, eh?'

He smiled at her apologetically and made as though to readjust the stack of drinks in order to go aboard. Gill's sense of relief was cut short as Tiffany clutched at Bart's arm.

'Don't just abandon me here!' she implored. 'I used my last cash in getting here on the strength of your application to the agency.'

She let her hand drop and half-turned away, her shoulders sagging as she added, 'I've no money left to take me anywhere else.'

Gill was sure it was a put-on act but she could see it was having an effect on Bart. He reached out his hand and caught hold of Tiffany's arm.

'Wait a minute,' he began.

Tiffany's face lit up again.

'I'll work for just my food and keep, if you'll take me on. Honestly! I just want to stay a while longer on this lovely island.'

Bart looked towards Gill and gave her a resigned shrug of his shoulders as he said, 'You can stay on trial, the same as Gill, and we'll see how it works out, but no promises, OK?'

'Terrific!' Tiffany squealed, grabbing hold of Bart and planting a kiss on his cheek. 'You won't regret it, I'm sure.'

No, but I might, Gill couldn't help reflecting inwardly.

'Gill will show you where to put your things,' Bart told Tiffany as he indicated that she go ahead of him aboard the catamaran. 'It'll be a bit of a tight squeeze in the cabin for you girls but it's only for sleeping in. I'm sure you'll manage. Show her where to put her things, Gill, and give her a quick tour. The passengers will be back soon and Wak and I need to get these cans stashed away.'

Gill turned smartly on her heels and led the way to the tiny cabin she was now to share with Tiffany.

'That's the galley,' she said, waving an airy hand towards it as they passed. 'This is the main cabin. Bart and Wak sleep here and it doubles as the dining-room and rest room whenever necessary. Washroom and toilet in here. Instructions for use are clearly written on the wall. This is our cabin.'

She had already decided that any swiftly-formed animosity had better be laid aside since they would be living in close contact so she turned and smiled at Tiffany.

'Is the top bunk OK for you?'

'Since you're asking, I'd prefer the lower bunk,' Tiffany replied with a toss of her head.

'That's fine. I'll change over,' Gill said lightly, determined to remain calm. 'And I'll empty this locker for you.'

'Only one?'

'There are only two available between us. Besides, you've only a small bag. There's plenty of room.'

'I like space.'

'Too bad! It was your choice to join the crew.'

'You're the one who shouldn't be here.'

'Well, I am here, so you'd better get

91

used to it. You should be thankful Bart agreed to take you on. He didn't have to. Look, Tiffany, don't you think we'd better make the best of the situation and at least try to get on together? Bart's depending on us to back him in his effort to make a go of these cruises. Silly squabbling won't help him, will it?'

'I don't know what you're talking about, I'm sure. I'll be indispensable to him before the day's out, so it's you who had better watch out.'

With that, Tiffany dropped her bag on the end of her bunk and pushed past Gill to leave the confined space of the cabin. With a rueful grimace, Gill followed her back on deck, uncomfortably aware that the hitherto spirit of harmony amongst the crew was unlikely to continue.

The passengers were returning along the jetty and as soon as they were on board, Bart gave orders to cast off. Before Gill could leap ashore to release one of the mooring ropes, Tiffany had beaten her to it, undoing the loops and leaping back on board with a practised expertise. Gill immediately took her station by one of the fenders and began to haul it aboard as soon as she saw Wak beginning at the other end.

'Are we raising the mainsail?' Tiffany called out.

'In a few minutes,' Bart replied. 'Stand-by for action.'

With a sinking heart, Gill recognised that Tiffany was well-used to sailing crafts and, as such, had a definite edge over her. If Bart had to make a choice between them, Tiffany would win hands down. Leaving her to it, Gill turned to the passengers, making sure they were settling themselves down again and offering drink to everyone. Rebecca and Mark launched into a tale of their time ashore, fully occupying her attention for a few minutes. When she had admired the souvenirs they had bought and then made sure they were safely stowed into their bags, she handed round plates of fruit.

After that, the guests were content to

alternate between sunbathing on deck and taking turns in the Jacuzzi. Tiffany's handling of the sails again showed her familiarity with sailing crafts as she leaped to obey Bart's commands, understanding immediately what was required of her. Even Wak was looking in danger of losing his job if he weren't careful.

Gill could only admire her talent, wondering how much it would sway Bart's decision if he had to make a choice between them. Philosophically, she shrugged her shoulders. She couldn't change the situation so why lose peace of mind over it?

'Come on, kids, tell me what you did ashore!'

She smiled at Rebecca and Mark, and Bart leaned against the mast, his eyes half-closed as he watched her listening to the children's chatter. Her eyes were sparkling with laughter and he remembered their underwater kiss and how her eyes seemed to caress him at times when she thought he wasn't looking. Now, they were teasing, but he wasn't sure whom she was teasing — the children or him! Maybe she was just a friendly girl who treated all the guys the same way. Time would tell if anything was to develop between them. He could wait.

He pushed himself away from the mast. Establishing his cruising business was his main concern and he didn't want to be distracted. Still . . . he cast a lingering look at her, aware that his pulse rate was quickening at the thought of her.

As if aware that his eyes were upon her, Gill looked up and met his gaze, still smiling at something one of the children had said to her. Not wanting to be drawn into revealing his thoughts, Bart merely nodded his approval at her easy rapport with the passengers, and he had turned away before the faint blush tinted Gill's cheeks.

Eventually, they left all sign of land behind them and Pegasus lived up to her name as she took on full sail, leaping through the water with effortless grace. It was exhilarating. Within half an hour, however, dark clouds were gathering behind them and Gill knew that the afternoon downpour was on its way.

'We'll outrun it at this speed,' Tiffany predicted confidently.

She was correct, and they had rounded the point of Datai Bay before the rain began to fall in huge droplets. Sheltered by the headland, the wind was less severe and the guests took temporary shelter in the main cabin until the sky cleared again to its brilliant blue.

Later, as they were taken ashore in the motor launch, every one of them was full of praise for the day's outing.

'Tell the other guests,' Bart said to them as he handed them out of the dinghy, knowing the value of word-of-mouth praise.

'We will!'

Pulling the dinghy up the beach, he followed the guests to the hotel, calling first at Reception to report on the success of the cruise and to learn of any bookings for the next day. He was pleased to hear that they would have a full complement of twelve, three young couples, a family with two teenage children and two young men.

Then he made his way to the kitchen to confirm his order for the following day's food, adjusting the amounts to suit the larger number of passengers. Sangkran was pleased to hear of his success.

'And I am pleased to see you looking much better, my friend.' Sangkran beamed at him. 'Did you discover anything about who might have assaulted you last evening?'

'No. Like you said, the conference party had already left. I don't suppose I'll ever know what happened, but I'd appreciate it if you kept your ears open for any relevant gossip among the staff. Someone must have seen something.'

On his return journey to the Pegasus, his thoughts turned to his two new crew members and he hoped that he wouldn't regret taking on both of them. There was no doubt that Tiffany knew all about boats and could handle one as well as he could himself. On the other hand, Gill was good with the passengers and seemed happy to put their comfort and enjoyment before her own.

Darkness had fallen with its usual speed whilst he had been inside the hotel but the moon was shining brightly and he could clearly see the outline of the catamaran. The tiny glow of a cigarette near the bow indicated that Wak was having a quiet time by himself. Bart grinned, knowing that the young man would be finding his two crewmates a bit of a handful. He'd have a drink with him after supper to boost his self-esteem.

All appeared quiet as he tied up the dinghy and climbed up the steps on to the deck, calling out a quiet greeting to Wak. Good! The girls had settled their differences and were no doubt having a girls' time together somewhere.

How wrong could he be!

'I am not your servant,' Gill's voice rang out angrily.

'I wouldn't employ you as one,' Tiffany cried back.

'Well, then, get your own drink. It's the only way you'll get one.'

'Girls! Girls!' Bart snapped as he strode forward. 'If you can't make up your minds to get on together, I'll be dropping both of you off at Kuah tomorrow. I'll do better without extra help.'

Of the two, Gill looked the more shamefaced as she looked from him to Tiffany. With a slight shrug of her shoulders, she spread out her hands, one of which was holding a canned drink.

'Yeah, well, you're right, I suppose. Only, I'd just finished tidying up and was going to sit on deck for a few minutes.'

She thrust the can towards Tiffany.

'Here, have this one. I'll get another.'

'No, thanks. I prefer a beer,' Tiffany refused, swinging towards the galley. 'I just thought that after all my hard work . . . '

'We all worked hard, Tiffany,' Bart pointed out. 'There are no strict demarcation lines between whose responsibility different tasks are. I expect everyone to pull together.'

He turned to Gill and asked, 'Is supper on the go?'

'Yes. Sorry, but it's more or less a repeat of lunch, but I've made some spicy fried rice to go with the meat and I've beaten some savoury batter to coat the prawns. Shall I get on with it now that you're back?'

'In a few minutes. Let's all sit on deck for a few minutes. Where's that beer, Tiffany?'

He stepped into the galley and was surprised to see Tiffany wiping the work surfaces.

'Good for you.' He nodded his approval.

'That's OK. I can't stand to see a place left in a mess,' Tiffany said lightly. 'That's how germs spread.'

'Too right. We can't be too careful in this climate. I expect Gill was coming back to it.'

Tiffany merely raised an eyebrow but didn't comment. She rinsed the cloth and draped it over the edge of the sink, and then took a canned beer out of the fridge.

'Here's your beer. Cheers!'

'Thanks. Get one for Wak, as well, won't you?'

They all sat on deck for half an hour, enjoying the balmy evening and conversing amicably. Gill slipped away quietly to the galley to put the finishing touches to their supper. Cooking was one of her pleasures and she didn't mind being the one designated to see to it. It had been Tiffany's casual insolence that had incensed her earlier and had stung her into making a stand.

The evening passed pleasantly enough. Bart went over the plan for the following day. It was to be a trip round the northern coast of the island to the north-east Tanjung Rhu Resort where the mangrove swamps were to be found and where the guests could hire kayaks, go paragliding, visit the Cave of Legends or swim from the magnificent beach. With a full complement of passengers, it promised to be a busy day.

6

Wakening early the next morning, Gill was determined to have a morning swim, hoping that nothing would curtail it like yesterday. The sun was already shining and, after rousing Tiffany to tell her where she was going, she hurried on deck. Wak was pulling himself up out of the water and grinned a greeting in return to hers.

'Where's Bart?' she asked as casually as she could.

She had found her thoughts of him disturbing her sleep and filling her waking moments, though she was honest enough with herself to wonder if her heightened awareness of him was because of the potential rivalry that Tiffany posed for his affections. Tiffany had openly flirted with him the previous evening.

She wasn't going to make a fool of

herself by competing for his affections in an undignified scramble. If all he wanted was transparent flattery, he wouldn't be getting it from her. Even so, when Wak, in response to her question, pointed behind and she could see Bart swimming strongly back towards the catamaran, her heart leaped in anticipation and she dived into the sea. Pretending to be amusing herself by swimming around and through the catamaran, she was very aware that Bart was drawing closer but was nonetheless taken by surprise when he surfaced suddenly just behind her and, his hands on her shoulders, drew her down into the depth of the sea.

This time, to her disappointment, he didn't attempt to kiss her underwater and, when they rose to the surface gasping for breath, he seemed more inclined to tease and frolic than to have any romantic inclinations, which was probably as well, as, within a few minutes, Tiffany's voice hailed from the deck and, having gained their attention, she executed a graceful dive into the sea.

The next thing Gill was aware of was that Bart was being pulled down beneath the surface, presumably by Tiffany. She saw him take a quick gulp of air before his face was submerged and she wondered sourly if he would attempt to kiss Tiffany whilst under the water, as he had her. She resisted the temptation of doing a surface dive to find out and, instead, swam round.

She saw that Bart was climbing up the short ladder back on to the catamaran. He turned at the top, holding up a hand with his fingers spread wide, presumably indicating to them to take no more than five minutes. Tiffany was pouting, no doubt in disappointment at Bart's early withdrawal from the scene. Gill waved her hand in acknowledgement and then smiled towards Tiffany in any attempt to have at least a semblance of friendship between them.

'Shall we swim twice round the boat

to give Bart time to shower?' she suggested.

'Suit yourself, I'll do a few dives and then get out.'

Having made the suggestion, Gill felt compelled to complete the two circuits and when she looked around after her second circuit, there was no sign of Tiffany, which made her last in the shower and thus the last ready for breakfast.

'Do help yourself,' Tiffany said sweetly, indicating the breakfast items set out on the table as Gill re-entered the main cabin. 'We're eating on deck.'

Gill was determined not to let the other girl tempt her into petty squabbling again. Her resolve nearly floundered when Tiffany manoeuvred herself into being the one to accompany Bart to the hotel to collect the barbecue ingredients and the guests but she was glad she hadn't said anything when Bart decided both girls could go.

'You go to Reception, Gill, and confirm our guest list, will you? I'll introduce Tiffany to Sangkran. Meet me in the kitchen in about five minutes.'

Gill confirmed the numbers and chatted easily to the girls on the desk for a few minutes before making her way down to the kitchen. By mistake, she stepped out of the lift at the wrong floor but, before she could step back inside, it had moved on. Seeing that it had been recalled to a higher floor, she decided to walk down the stairs to the lower floor to save time.

Set as it was in the lower slopes of the jungle, the hotel had open passageways and staircases and as Gill began to descend the first half of the staircase that led down to the ground floor, she could hear two voices in quiet conversation drifting up from the floor below.

Hearing the female voice say, 'Don't worry, I'll do it today,' Gill froze. Was it Tiffany? The other voice wasn't Bart's, so, if it was Tiffany, whom did she know at the hotel? Gill didn't like eavesdropping but couldn't help wanting to be certain who was speaking. A chattering sound from the ground to her right drew her attention and she could see some monkeys scampering across the grassy area among some shrubs that surrounded the hotel. The female speaker squealed and laughed and darted to the wooden balcony rail.

Gill drew back. It was Tiffany! She was pushing something blue into her pocket and, when her companion stepped forward to join her at the rail, Gill recognised him as being the same man with whom she had spoken briefly the previous morning. She frowned. How did Tiffany know him, and did it matter? After all, she herself had spoken to him, and she didn't know him. Surely she was being super-sensitive, seeing problems before they existed.

Even if it were nonsense, she didn't want them to know that she had lingered to listen to their conversation and so she turned and ran back up the stairs. She knew that there was another staircase down to the ground floor at the far end of the open passageway and she hurried along to it. By the time she reached the kitchen she was slightly out of breath but was relieved to see that Bart was still there, discussing the menu with Sangkran.

'Ah, there you are! I thought you'd got lost,' Bart greeted her. 'I sent Tiffany to find you. Did you see her?'

'I got out of the lift on the wrong floor,' Gill excused herself.

She was evading Bart's direct question, still not sure why she was being evasive. She just didn't trust Tiffany, or was she simply jealous of her? She didn't know.

'Not to worry,' Bart commented. 'What are the numbers for today?'

'Twelve, just as you said.'

'Good.'

He turned to Sangkran.

'The amounts are fine then. Thanks, Sangkran. You're a great help.'

'Any time, my friend.'

Apart from the two teenagers, the average age of the passengers was in the early-to-mid thirties, so it was altogether a different atmosphere from the previous day. The three couples made straight for the deck and the firm netted area at the bow and swiftly organised themselves for sunbathing. The family, with a boy of about thirteen and a girl who looked about sixteen, organised themselves a bit more slowly but gradually sorted out some space for themselves.

Gill busied herself providing drinks for everyone, leaving Tiffany to dazzle the two young men with her seafaring skills. It was an area she couldn't compete in. Bart issued a few orders. Wak and Tiffany hauled on a few ropes. The sails began to rise and flap noisily as they caught the wind and Pegasus shivered into life.

The sails filled out and Gill caught her breath as the boat leaped forward, slicing through the water on its twin hulls. This was the life, she exulted.

It was a busy, exciting day. All of the passengers who wished to sample the high-speed Jacuzzi did so and by the time they were dropping anchor at Tanjung Rhu, it was time for Gill to begin to prepare the lunch. The passengers had the choice of hiring kayaks for an hour or to go paragliding.

Bart delegated Tiffany to accompany those wishing to hire kayaks, confident that she would be able to give any helpful advice to guests if they needed it. Wak took them ashore first and then brought the dinghy back for the others.

'You're sure you can manage the barbecue, Gill?' Bart asked as he prepared to accompany the six passengers who were going to risk life and limb paragliding. 'I'll send Wak back to give you a hand if you wish.'

'No, I'll be fine,' Gill assured him. 'Go on and enjoy yourself. Are you going up?'

'Not this time. I've got to make sure our guests all get a turn.'

He moved closer and lifted her chin with an extended finger.

'Shall I book a tandem harness for a

future occasion?'

Gill felt her heart stop beating, whether caused by the challenge or by his touch, she wasn't sure. Did he know the effect that the closeness of his body had on her? She swallowed hard as a ripple of desire coursed through her and forced a casual note into her voice.

'I'll take a rain-check on that one!'

'Not scared, are you?'

His eyes were laughing and Gill felt a sense of annoyance rise within her.

'No!' she snapped, jerking her head away from him. 'I've nothing to prove, that's all.'

Bart laughed and prepared to climb down into the dinghy.

'We'll see about that,' he said, adding as he reached the dinghy, 'Don't start cooking the meat until you see Wak bringing the first boatload back again. Nobody will mind waiting a while. They can always have a swim.'

Gill watched as the dinghy went ashore, wondering what were Bart's true feelings for her. They had only known each other for two days but she felt as though she had known him for ever. She wondered if it would be different if they were both holiday-makers with opportunities to stroll hand in hand along the shore and time to relax and have a proper holiday romance. But, what use were holiday romances? They usually fizzled out with the inevitable separation at the airport. At least, with a bit of luck, she would have a few weeks of working alongside Bart, during which time their friendship could develop more slowly.

Satisfied with her thoughts, Gill turned her mind to her task in hand. When everything was checked and ready for their barbecue, she still had half an hour or so for a spot of sunbathing.

The sound of the outboard motor alerted her to the return of the first boatload and by the time they were climbing aboard, she was ready to offer the various thirst quenchers.

'Quite the little hostess, aren't you?'

Tiffany sneered as she took a glass off the tray. 'Pity you can't do the real stuff. Bart will soon be getting rid of you, I can tell you.'

'Says who?' Gill quipped, unmoved by Tiffany's jibe. 'An army marches on its stomach, and so do holidaymakers.'

'Hey, girls, any drinks coming round?' one of the young men called out.

Tiffany turned with a dazzling smile, taking the tray out of Gill's hands before Gill realised what she was doing.

'Sure thing, boys. Coming right away. Back to the galley, you,' she mouthed over her shoulder.

Gill hoped Tiffany would slip on the deck. Fuming at her insolence, Gill went to start up the barbecue.

'Want any help?' Ian, one of the single men asked.

'Pardon? Oh, yes. That would be great. Thanks.' Gill smiled. 'Set these chicken legs on the grill, will you? I'll get the fish next and one of you can keep an eye on the wok with the chilli fried prawns.'

She grinned to herself as the other men drifted over to the barbecue, attracted by the appetising aroma. When she returned to the galley to collect a second wok, she was surprised to collide with Tiffany, who was just emerging. Gill didn't like the smug expression on the other girl's face.

'What are you up to?' she asked.

'Just getting another drink!' Tiffany replied, waving a can in Gill's face. 'I don't need your permission, do I?'

Gill didn't bother to reply. She picked up the second wok and took it out to her willing helpers at the barbecue.

'What's that?' Will, another of the men, asked.

'Beef Rendang. The sauce has been reduced in cooking, so it's quite thick. Keep it moving then it won't stick.'

She returned to the galley to begin to put out the cold salads and sauces, aware that the dinghy had returned again. The timing was good. The meal was almost ready.

Bart joined her in the main cabin as she set out the side dishes.

'You've got a keen gang of would-be chefs out there.'

He was carrying in a large platter of the cooked chicken legs, which he jostled into place among the other dishes.

'And not an arm twisted.' Gill grinned at him.

'I'm not sure it's a good idea,' Tiffany commented as she followed Bart into the cabin, picking up a chicken leg and biting into it. 'You can't be too careful with food.'

'I've no problem with it, Tiffany,' Bart refuted her comment. 'The guests often like to help, especially with a barbecue. Part of our success is because of our informal approach. Oh, and let the guests fill their plates first before we start. There'll be plenty left for us to have a go at later.'

'Well, don't say I didn't warn you,' Tiffany snapped as she flounced outside, tossing the chicken on to a work surface as she passed the galley.

Gill shrugged, glad that Bart had backed her but sorry to have any hint of discord among the crew whilst passengers were on board. However, Tiffany had obviously put aside her critical attitude and was flirting with the men at the barbecue when Gill went out to see if the rest of the food was ready.

'Five minutes, everyone,' she called out. 'Come and get your drinks.'

The guests made hearty inroads into the sumptuous spread and were very appreciative with their comments. Bart was certainly on to a winner with his cruises, Gill surmised. With the tropical climate, interesting places to visit by water and excellent food, there wasn't much to complain about.

After the crew had eaten and the guests were ready to relax sunbathing or in the Jacuzzi, Bart suggested that Gill should clear away the remnants of the food and tidy up whilst the rest of the crew got the catamaran under sail once more.

They were now entering the mangrove swamps where the spectacular root formations of the trees were admired and the sight of metre-long monitor lizards exclaimed over. A visit to the Cave of Legends brought an end to the passive after-lunch interlude and Bart offered the guests the choice of reversing the morning activities of kayaking or paragliding or, alternatively, the opportunity to bathe from the Tanjung Rhu Resort beach.

'And you and I can go paragliding,' he whispered softly in Gill's ear.

Before Gill was given the opportunity to test her nerve, events took a downturn when several of the guests began to complain of stomach pains and were scuttling, one after the other, to the resort's public conveniences.

Bart had to face the fact that, somehow or other, most of his passengers were suffering from some form of food poisoning.

7

Fortunately, none of the passengers was vomiting and, after an hour's discomfort, most of them were feeling well enough to face the short sail by dinghy to the catamaran. Of the crew, only Tiffany complained of feeling ill and, of the passengers, only Simon, the teenage boy, escaped the bug.

After settling the guests either on deck or in the cabin, wherever they wished to go, Gill served drinks of bottled water. None of the guests was too loud in their complaining but it was clear that the earlier happy atmosphere had been lost from and Gill heard murmurings of the possibility of them asking for a discount as means of compensation. That made Gill's heart sink. It would hit Bart's budget hard. The crew then retreated to gather by the wheelhouse where they could talk in some degree of privacy.

'Surely they would be vomiting if it were food poisoning,' Gill reasoned.

'Not necessarily,' Bart argued. 'It might be from the water. Did you use our pumped water to wash the salads?'

'No, they were all ready-prepared.'

'Just checking. It's got to have come from somewhere.'

'I told you it was risky letting the passengers help with the cooking,' Tiffany reminded them. 'That, or Gill's been too slap-happy with her own hygiene. I told you the galley's always in a mess.'

'No, it isn't!' Gill protested. 'I wipe down all the cupboard surfaces after breakfast and again before starting on lunch. Anyway, why aren't we ill? We've eaten the same as the guests, haven't we?'

'Possibly. Is there anything we three didn't eat?' Bart's glance included Gill and Wak. 'There must be something. If Tiffany hadn't shown signs of the symptoms, I might have thought it could be a delayed reaction from something at the Andaman. You didn't eat anything whilst we were there this morning, did you, Tiffany?'

'No, of course not! I was with you in the kitchen and I didn't go anywhere near the restaurant.'

'What about you, Wak?'

Wak shook his head.

'I think I eat some of everything,' he admitted.

'I didn't eat any of the Beef Rendang,' Gill remembered. 'It had all gone, so I removed the dish, and that was before you came to eat, Wak, so you didn't have any either. I think I had some of everything else. What about you, Bart?'

'Same here,' Bart agreed. 'The dish had gone. So, can you remember if you had any beef, Tiffany?'

Tiffany shrugged. 'I really couldn't say. Let's face it. It could have been anything or everything. You know my opinion.'

Gill's cheeks flushed red.

'The galley is perfectly clean,' she snapped. 'The fridge, the surfaces, the lot. You are just trying to stir up trouble.'

'The facts speak for themselves,' Tiffany snapped back. 'Someone on this boat has careless hygiene habits.'

'Well, it's not me, honestly, Bart. I did everything by the book.'

'OK! OK! Let's not get too personal about it, Tiffany,' Bart said, trying to keep everyone calm. 'We don't know the cause yet, but there's bound to be an enquiry. We'll have to keep all the waste-food bags. No doubt they'll have to be sent off for analysis.'

His face was sombre.

'This could close us down, you know. The hotel won't want any slurs on its reputation.'

'What if the contamination came from the food company?' Gill suggested. 'That would let us off the hook, wouldn't it?'

'But not in time for tomorrow,' Bart pointed out. 'Look, girls, I'm sorry, but without money coming in, I won't be able to keep either of you on. Just to survive, I'll have to hope to get some casual sea-trips without food provided, and even that may prove impossible, depending what restrictions the authorities slap on me.'

His glance rested more on Gill than on Tiffany and Gill wondered if he were trying to tell her that it mattered to him. She felt sick at heart to think of his business failing before it had had the chance to get properly off the ground, especially because of something like this. Had she been at fault in any way? She couldn't think how.

'Oh, well, easy come, easy go!' Tiffany dismissed the matter lightly. 'Maybe you should drop off the passengers and sail into the sunset as fast as you can. There are plenty of other places to run a boat business.'

Bart raised an eyebrow at her suggestion.

'Is that what you would do, Tiffany?'

'Why not? You could set up somewhere else. What does it matter?'

'It would matter to me, Tiffany. There's such a thing as integrity.'

'Well, yes. Anyway, I wasn't really serious.' Tiffany tried to laugh it off. 'I was just trying to think of some alternatives for you.'

Gill had a sudden thought.

'What had you planned for tomorrow, Bart? Wasn't it the diving and snorkelling platform at Palua Payar?'

Bart ran a distracted hand through his hair.

'Yes. It should have been a good trip. We've had a lot of interest shown in it, according to Reception. Pity!'

'Doesn't the advertising leaflet mention a public buffet lunch on the platform?'

'That's right. It's not bad, but I intended to keep with our more exclusive buffet for the hotel guests. Still . . .'

A glimmer of hope began to gleam in his eyes.

'It's worth a try. Thanks, Gill.'

'Ooh, Little Miss Goody!' Tiffany mocked.

'Whatever, she may have just saved your jobs,' Bart pointed out.

The guests were a subdued bunch as they were ferried in three batches to the hotel beach. Gill accompanied Bart on the first dinghy-load, so that she could make a report about her usual precautionary hygiene in the kitchen. The duty manager was called and was understandably perturbed by the incident, although not as condemnatory as Gill feared.

'There is always a risk in climates such as ours, especially when the guests eat away from the hotel in places where we have no control,' he commented. 'No-one has complained throughout the day, so it looks as though it may be confined to your catamaran. I'm afraid it means we can't allow you to continue to run your sea-trips from here. Our first duty is to our hotel guests. I'm sorry. There has been a lot of interest shown.'

He glanced down at a list on the desk.

'You had another full complement for tomorrow's trip. I'll get someone to notify them at once.'

'Before you do that, Mr Ibrahim, would you consider letting us run the trips without us providing food until we know the cause of the incident?'

Bart pulled out the leaflet that advertised the public buffet on Palua Payar and indicated the item.

'If you agree, I'll be able to modify all the trips I had planned, making sure that we're near public eating places at lunchtimes.'

Gill held her breath as Mr Ibrahim considered the idea, praying inwardly that he would decide in their favour. She fixed her eyes on his face, trying to read his thoughts from his expression. To her great relief, he eventually smiled his assent.

'I don't see why not. You'll have to reduce the prices accordingly, of course, so you won't be making as much profit, but it will keep the door open for you here, depending on the results of the food-waste analysis. Yes, I'll go with that for the time being, as long as you serve only bottled and canned drinks and fruit that your guests can peel themselves.'

They handed over the plastic waste bag and pointed out the separate bag containing the scraped remains of the Beef Rendang as being the most likely culprit.

Mr Ibrahim thanked them for their co-operation, adding, 'When you ring your food supplier to cancel your orders, ask if there have been any other complaints. You never know, that might take the onus off you. In the meantime, I'll have to send someone over immediately to take swabs from your kitchen equipment and surfaces.'

Gill had to almost run to keep up with Bart as he strode back to the beach. He seemed deep in thought.

'Bart, I really am sorry about this,' she apologised. 'I truly don't know how it happened. I know it must be connected with the food but I don't know how. I wasn't careless with hygiene. I know I wasn't.'

He slowed his pace and turned to face her. His eyes seemed to have regained some of their usual warmth and Gill's heart began to thump erratically. Maybe he didn't hold her responsible for the unhappy incident. Bart reached out and touched her arm, drawing her to a standstill. His fingers seemed to sear her flesh and she gasped as she raised her eyes to meet his, immediately aware once more of his sensuality and the sheer magnetic appeal he held for her. When he spoke, his voice was flat but his words raised Gill's spirit a little.

'Even if it proves to be cross contamination, Gill, it doesn't mean it's got to be you. We all use the galley. It could be any one of us.'

Gill felt some degree of comfort. At least he wasn't blaming her out of hand. Without meaning to, she stepped closer to him and found that her hands had risen to rest against his chest. She could feel his heartbeat and the

128

closeness of their bodies caused a catch in her breathing. She wanted to comfort him, to give him hope, but didn't know how. In happier circumstances she felt he would have kissed her but, somehow, it seemed inappropriate.

Instead, she drew her head back slightly and asked, 'Will it mean a great loss to you, not being able to offer food to the passengers?'

Bart pulled a wry expression.

'More than fifty per cent. Basic food produce is relatively cheap here, so there's good profit in high-quality catering. It won't be an actual loss because I won't be paying out for the food items, but the profit will be down. We'll have to pull our belts in, which reminds me, what have we got in the fridge or store cupboard for supper and breakfast?'

'Not much, I'm afraid. Muesli, eggs and fruit and what's left of the canned drinks.'

'We won't starve. However, I'd better

fix up a deal with the hotel for a basic breakfast and cheap supper for us for the next few days.'

He dropped a very light kiss on the top of her head and, in unspoken accord, they continued towards the beach, now with their arms companionably around each other's waist. Looking down at her, Bart hugged her closer.

'Don't look so sad. We'll be OK. We'll manage.'

Wak was waiting for them and they were soon back on board the catamaran. Tiffany was in the galley. For a moment, Gill thought she was making supper but all Tiffany had in her hand was a packet of sugar.

'Er . . . I thought I'd make some coffee,' she said quickly, as if she thought she had to explain being in the kitchen. 'I suppose you'll all want some.'

Gill glanced around suspiciously, unable to accept Tiffany's offer at face value. However, nothing seemed out of place and she relaxed, managing a conciliatory smile.

'Since you're offering, thanks. I'll make us an omelette later, if you like.'

'No thanks! I don't fancy eating on board any more.'

Gill shrugged.

'Please yourself. There's a bag of muesli and some left-over fruit. You'll have to make do with that.'

However, when a food official contacted by the hotel sped out from the hotel beach in a motor-launch, he brought with him a wrapped-up parcel of hot-food containers filled with vegetables, curried meats and rice, all of which were a gift from Sangkran.

'Sit on deck and eat,' he bade them. 'That will leave everywhere free for me to take my samples. After I've gone, give everywhere a good scrub down with the liquid in those orange bottles I brought and I'll come out to take more samples tomorrow. Don't serve any food on board until I've given you the all-clear.'

'What about muesli and fruit juices

straight from packets?' Gill asked.

'For your own consumption?'

'Yes.'

'That's fine. No raw meats or dairy foods though.'

The man got on with his work efficiently, leaving Bart and his crew to enjoy their supper. After the man had departed, they all set to and scrubbed down the boat. It was hard work and no-one objected when Bart called a halt and suggested everyone went to bed. It was to be an early start the following day.

★ ★ ★

Bart ferried the new party of guests to the boat, twelve in all, making the announcement about the change in eating plans like an unexpected treat. He had cleared the details with the catering firm who ran the buffet lunch on the diving platform and assured the passengers that they were in for a good treat. Once they were all aboard and

132

settled on deck with a drink in their hands, Bart set Wak and Tiffany into action hauling up the sails and Pegasus sprang into life.

'Huh! It's a day off for you,' Tiffany tossed at Gill when she found her relaxing on the foredeck. 'I wouldn't be surprised to find that you had deliberately planned it all for an easy life.'

'Don't talk ridiculously, Tiffany,' Gill responded, trying to keep her voice even. 'I wouldn't be stupid enough as to do myself out of a job. I'm hoping we'll be back in action in a few days.'

'Don't count on it,' Tiffany hissed, her eyes narrowed.

In spite of the heat, Gill felt a chill run through her.

'What do you mean?'

'You'll see!'

Tiffany sauntered to the netting spread over the water, joining the small group of passengers who were sun-bathing there, leaving Gill to gaze after her, wondering what the other girl was up to.

They had a wonderful day. Because there were no meals to prepare, Bart told the crew to join in the activities. Wak preferred to stay on duty on board the catamaran so Bart and the two girls kitted themselves out with flippers, life-jackets and snorkelling equipment and joined in the fun.

Tiffany entered the water quickly and swam off with some of their single men passengers. Gill was relieved to see her go, still feeling uneasy about her remarks earlier on. She wondered whether to mention what she had said to Bart but decided against it. It was probably all talk, wanting to stir Gill's peace of mind and Gill did her best to completely forget about their problems and enjoy herself.

It was the first time she had had the opportunity to snorkel in deep water and found it exhilarating to be swimming among so many brightly-coloured fish that seemed to have no fear of their presence. Once she had got the hang of it, Bart grabbed hold of Gill's hand and towed her alongside him, pointing out with his outstretched hand more and more exotic fish. He handed her a pinch of something, pellets of bread, she surmised, and watched in delight as some of the fish swam right up to her.

Being in such close contact with Bart was a delight in itself and the break for lunch came round too quickly. After lunch, passengers were taken in small groups in some glass-bottomed boats across to a separate section where young sharks were being fed. The time sped by. Before there was time to grow tired of swimming among the fish, Bart signalled by tapping on his wrist that it was time for them to finish for the day.

'We'll get showered and changed before our passengers,' he told her. 'Then you can be ready with some cold drinks and hand round the basket of fruit. Go and get your shampoo and odds and ends and take advantage of the showers on the platform whilst they are still available.'

Bart spotted Tiffany and signalled to her to come also before he followed Gill up the short gang-plank to board Pegasus. Gill hurried into her small cabin to grab hold of her toiletries bag and rushed straight out again, her hand rummaging in the contents for her bottle of shampoo. Head down, she didn't see Bart until she collided with him in the doorway of the main cabin, dropping her bag on to the floor.

'Oops! Sorry!' she apologised, bending down to pick up everything.

Bart was there before her, scooping up the contents.

'What do you females cram into your bags?' he teased. 'Just look at it all. Toothpaste and brush, shampoo, scent, nail scissors, and what's this?'

His face changed as he read the label on the outside of a flat blue plastic box. Gill's breath caught in her throat. The box wasn't hers. What was it doing in her bag? Her eyes narrowed as her mind jumped back to the previous morning and a fleeting image of Tiffany pushing something blue into her bag when she was talking to that man sped into her inner vision.

'It's . . . '

'I can read what it is, Gill!' Bart's voice said coldly. 'It's a packet of strong laxatives, empty, of course! So, that's what happened yesterday. How could you, Gill?'

8

Bart! It's not mine!' Gill croaked, her voice hurting in her tightened throat. She felt the blood drain out of her face, leaving it stiff with shock. 'I don't know how it got into my bag but it's not mine. Honestly!'

Bart felt sick. How could he have been so wrong about anyone? He forced himself to look at her.

'Honesty doesn't seem to have much meaning to you, Gill, does it? You lied to get taken on board as crew, you've lied in all your seeming offers of help! What else have you lied about? Just what is your game?'

They were both crouching down in the cabin doorway but Bart took hold of her arm tightly and pulled her upright, his other hand waving the box accusingly before her.

'Why, Gill, why?'

'Quarrelling already?' Tiffany's voice cut in.

'It's hers! Tiffany's the one who made the guests ill!' Gill accused. 'I saw her with it!'

'Saw me with what?' Tiffany asked, pushing her way into the cabin.

'This box! That man at the hotel gave it to you. I saw him.'

Tiffany tossed back her hair.

'I don't know what you're talking about.' She peered at the box. 'I haven't seen it before, and I've no idea which man you are talking about. What's it all about?'

'Don't lie, Tiffany,' Gill cried. 'You know very well what the box contained. You somehow mixed it in yesterday's food. You made all the guests ill. You're trying to ruin Bart's business, aren't you?'

'Liar, yourself! Why should I make the guests ill when you're doing such a good job of it? Besides, I was ill myself, remember? I wouldn't have made myself ill, would I?'

'We've only your word on that, and I don't reckon much to your word.'

Gill remembered the jibe Tiffany had flung at her on the outward journey.

'This is what you meant earlier, isn't it? When I said we would soon be back in action and you said, 'Don't count on it!''

Tiffany stood with her hands on her hips, her face full of scorn.

'I really have no idea what you are talking about. Admit it! You've been found out, and none too soon, if you ask me.'

'Stop it, girls,' Bart commanded, his face dark and forbidding, his eyes gleaming as cold as ice. 'The guests will be back on board soon and I'm not having them listening to the pair of you accusing each other. As far as I can see, either of you could have done it. You've both had the opportunity to either contaminate the food or to plant the evidence. Well, I've had enough. I'm diverting our homeward run to Kuah, and you'll both leave us.'

'No!'

It was Gill whose anguished voice whispered the denial. Her face had flooded red during the confrontation with Tiffany, but now it blanched white again. She couldn't bear it. Tiffany merely tossed back her hair.

'So, what? I don't care! I'll soon get another job, better paid than this!'

★ ★ ★

Gill stood disconsolately on the jetty at Kuah watching Pegasus shrink smaller and smaller until it was lost from her sight. Even then, she couldn't bring herself to turn away. He'd come back for her, he would. She had seen the hurt in his eyes. It was as hard for him as it was for her.

But he didn't come back. He couldn't really, could he? He had to get his passengers back to the hotel. Had he told them what had happened? Did everyone believe that she had schemed to ruin Bart's business?

Well, one thing she knew for certain, it wasn't her! And, by logical reason, it had to be Tiffany who wanted to ruin Bart. But, why? What did she have against him?

Gill turned to stare down the road that led into the town. Tiffany had long since taken herself off towards the town, a self-satisfied smile on her face. Gill had been glad to see her go and wanted to allow some distance to pass between them. Now, she remembered the man she had seen Tiffany speaking with and her thoughts shot along a different route. Tiffany was only the messenger of trouble. The real culprit was someone else, the same man or the dark-haired man she had seen him meet on her first day.

Even so, what did they hope to gain by putting Bart out of business? He wasn't exactly a shipping tycoon! He owned one boat, not even that, she remembered. His grandfather owned it. It would only become Bart's if he made a success of his venture.

She stared out to sea thoughtfully. Was that it? What would happen to the boat if Bart failed? Bart hadn't said. And, anyway, it was a bit fanciful. She was probably looking for demons where there weren't any.

She sighed deeply. It hadn't occurred to Bart that the last ferry to Penang had already left. She had better find somewhere cheap to stay for the night and put her brain into action about what to do next. She didn't want to limp back to England with her tail between her legs but, on the other hand, could she bear to stay on Langkawi without Bart? Her throat tightened and she felt tears threatening to prick her eyes. She determinedly shook them away. No man was going to make her cry!

She stooped down to pick up her rucksack and slung it over her shoulder. If her memory served her well, the tourist office was about a kilometre from the jetty, not that the office would be open but there was a chance there could be a list of accommodation posted in the window, maybe, even some jobs vacancies.

With a superficial jauntiness, Gill strode along. The sky was darkening visibly. The afternoon rainfall was coming late today and before Gill was anywhere near the tourist office, the rain was bouncing off the roads and pavements. Gill dived into the nearest open doorway to take shelter, trying to shake the rain out of her hair and off her clothes. The downpour wouldn't last long and she would soon dry out.

She poked her head out of the doorway and realised that two doors along the street was a café. She made a rapid calculation of the money she had left and decided that the cost of a drink would only make a tiny dent in her purse. She held her rucksack over her head in preparation of dashing along the street but, after taking one step outside, she darted back into the doorway. Tiffany and a man wearing dark spectacles were hurrying across the road and into the café! Was he the man from the hotel? She wasn't sure.

Thank goodness they hadn't seen her!

Tiffany must have got in touch with her accomplice immediately and he had come to meet her here. It would be interesting to hear what they were saying to each other. Dare she try? She knew she had to! She waited a few minutes, to give them time to settle themselves and then she carefully approached the café, hoping they would be too engrossed in each other to notice her.

They weren't the only customers dashing in out of the rain and a smiling Malaysian boy met her just beyond the doorway and asked her to wait.

'Just a few minutes, miss. I soon have a place for you. You wait here?'

'That's fine,' she agreed quietly, lowering her rucksack to the floor.

She tried to peer into the dim interior. Where were they? Could she somehow get near to them without being seen? Her attention was grabbed by a female voice the other side of a painted screen that sheltered the interior of the café from the outside elements. She couldn't believe her luck! It was Tiffany! Gill unashamedly bent her head towards the screen to listen.

'It was easy! No-one suspected a thing until it was too late.'

'But with you out of the picture, we'll have to get someone else aboard to finish Lawson. You shouldn't have been so obviously antagonistic to the girl. Lawson won't be quite so ready to take on a new crew member,' her male companion said sharply.

He was the man from the hotel! She recognised his voice.

'Dan isn't going to like it!'

Who was Dan? The other man she had seen at the hotel?

'No sweat! I've fixed him. He'll be out of action long enough to let Dan take over with his boat. He won't get back in again. The Andaman will be fed-up with him letting them down so often.'

'What did you do?'

'It was child's play. I just did this.'

Tiffany laughed and Gill frowned, wondering what action had accompanied her words. Before she had time to let her imagination work on it, Tiffany's voice continued.

'Bart was careless enough to leave me on board for an hour by myself. I hope it happens when he's running ahead of a storm. That'll give him something to worry about.'

The man laughed unpleasantly.

'I'll give Dan a ring. He can be getting the Pelican ready to come sailing out of the sunset.'

'But when are you going to tell me what it's all about?' Tiffany demanded. 'I've been risking my neck, whilst all you do is sit back and give orders. When are you going to pay me? I got nothing off Bart, you know, only enough money for a night's lodgings and to get me to the mainland. I could

147

make things awkward for you and this Dan you talk about. I'm sure Bart would be interested to learn who has been causing his little mishaps.'

'Yes, you are quite right, my dear. We'd better get on the phone to Dan and see what he thinks you're worth. No, not on a mobile. It could be traced. I know where some public phones are. Let's go. Waiter!'

Gill had heard enough. She couldn't risk being in the doorway when Tiffany and her companion came out and she could see the waiter approaching them. He would be inviting her to their vacated table any second. She picked up her rucksack and slipped outside, being careful to retreat the way she had come, away from the café window. Somehow, she must warn Bart that something on his boat had been sabotaged. Did he have a mobile phone? She hadn't seen him use one.

Pushing communication problems aside, she concentrated on concealing herself from view when Tiffany and her companion came out. If they were going to a public phone booth, she could follow them at a distance and make use of it herself once they were safely out of the area. If she were to telephone the hotel, she could ask to speak to Sangkran, the only person she knew by name whom she felt she could trust.

She slipped around the corner of the next street and into the first doorway. Thankfully, it was still raining and her action wouldn't look too strange to any passerby. She flattened herself against the side of the window, her back towards the street, her ears straining to hear approaching footsteps. She heard Tiffany's voice and her body tensed but the footsteps came no nearer and she realised that they were crossing the top of the street where she was hiding. Giving them a few seconds to cross the road, she risked a careful peep through the double layers of glass windows and caught a glimpse of the two conspirators just as they were lost to sight.

Hoping nothing would cause them to turn around, she hurried across the road and sped to the corner. A cautious glance showed they were just turning into the next street. Gill frowned a little, wondering why the man seemed to look different from the back. His hair was darker and longer. But it had been his voice at the hotel, she was certain. Had he felt the need to change his appearance whilst in town? What was it all about?

She hurried along the pavement. The farther away from the main street they went, the surroundings were deteriorating rapidly and she was beginning to feel a sense of alarm rising within. Surely any public phone booths would be in the town centre.

Her breath caught in her throat as she wondered if they knew she was following them and were leading her into a trap. She quickly side-stepped into the next doorway and backed against the wall, breathing deeply to try to calm herself. A sharp, explosive report caused her eyes to fly wide open as her body froze. Her mind refused to accept what her senses had heard. A gunshot? No, it had to be something else.

She glanced around the edge of the brickwork at her side and sharply drew in her breath.

Tiffany lay in a crumpled heap in the roadway!

9

Gill's mind seemed to move forward in a series of stills — Tiffany on the ground; the man darting around the next corner; various people slowly emerging from doorways and moving towards Tiffany; a shout of alarm; someone darting into a building.

Gill found herself being drawn forward as if by a magnetic force beyond her control. There had to be some mistake. Things like this didn't happen to people you knew. Maybe Tiffany had simply tripped and fallen. The sound could have been something else, an exhaust back-firing.

As she drew closer, she knew it was no mistake. The expressions on the faces of the gathering crowd showed that, and from the shaking of heads, Gill knew that Tiffany was dead. A sudden panic gripped her as the realisation of what had happened sank in. The man had deliberately brought Tiffany into this downtown back street and had shot her in cold blood, and then disappeared. It had been a premeditated act.

Where was he now? Was he already far away from the scene before anyone could recognise him and connect him with the shooting? The man's changed appearance suddenly made sense. If anyone remembered seeing Tiffany in the café, she had been with a man with long dark hair and dark spectacles. With those swiftly removed, there would be nothing in his real appearance to connect him with Tiffany.

A chill swept through Gill's body. Was he lingering somewhere to see what would happen? If he were brazen enough, he could casually walk upon the scene and pretend shock and horror at the callous murder. Gill shrank within herself. If he were to see her, he would swiftly suspect that she had witnessed part of the incident and, from the brutality shown to Tiffany, he would have no hesitation in meting out something similar to her.

But what should she do?

Back home, there would be no problem. She would step forward as a witness of Tiffany's identity, if nothing more, for she hadn't actually seen the murder, but she had no idea of Malaysian police procedure. Apart from the language difficulty, would they believe her? And, even if they did, would they react in time? Going forward to identify Tiffany wouldn't help Tiffany in any way. She was beyond such help, whereas Bart was in real danger and she needed to warn him immediately.

So, fighting her inner instinct, Gill melted back into the crowd, keeping her head down. No-one seemed to connect her with the body on the ground. Even so, she was terrified of anyone stopping her or, worse still, of bumping into Tiffany's assailant. She could be running straight into his path.

All she could think was that she needed to contact Bart and the only person she felt she could trust as a mediator was Sangkran. She needed a telephone, fast. Surprisingly, she found herself back in the main street, though nowhere near the café where she had seen Tiffany. At the thought of Tiffany, Gill sensed a surge of panic again. No matter how the girl had plotted against Bart, she hadn't deserved to be killed like that.

What sort of organisation was Bart up against that they could so ruthlessly execute one of their number, someone who, presumably, was no longer of any use to them? Maybe Tiffany's hint of blackmail or reprisal had sealed her fate. Whatever, it was still cold-hearted and cruel.

Gill shivered. Her clothes were soaked and her hair hung around her face. The rain had stopped and people were emerging from the various shops and cafés. Normal life was continuing around her. It didn't seem right. It made what had happened back there seem insignificant, unreal. Had it really happened? But, of course, she knew it had.

She needed to calm down and think. Her main problem was time. It was now late afternoon. Dusk would be upon them soon and she didn't want to be stranded in Kuah after nightfall. She had to make that phone call. She spotted a nearby café. It might have a public phone.

Her hesitant enquiries brought a smile of assent to the bartender's face.

'Yes, missy. Telephone through there. You have drink of coffee, yes?'

'Yes, please.' She needed a hot drink. 'I'll make my call whilst you make it,' she suggested, moving in the direction the man had indicated.

When she got through to the hotel, it was to learn that Sangkran wasn't on duty that evening. She didn't want to leave a message. For all she knew, Tiffany's accomplice might be an employee at the hotel. He might soon be back there, unless his purpose had ended with Tiffany's death. No, it was Bart they were after. He was still in danger. What now?

Struggling to hold herself together, she realised she had two options. Kuah was as far from the hotel as it could possibly be, situated as they were at opposite ends of the island. She could either try to get to the Andaman to contact Bart that way, or, she could stay overnight in Kuah and hope that Bart called at the jetty the following morning to stock up on drinks.

Either way held risks of failure. She might not be able to gain access to Bart even if she reached the Andaman. Dusk was falling and it would soon be pitch dark. Similarly, she might miss Bart's call at the jetty the following day, and, depending on what form the sabotage took, it might already be too late by then, And, another thought, they might try some other means to be rid of him. The ruthless killing of Tiffany showed that they were determined in their task, whatever it was.

Gill sipped her hot coffee. The thought of sleeping in some fourth-rate accommodation and then missing Bart as well didn't appeal one little bit. If she took a taxi to the Andaman Hotel, she would arrive there whilst it was still early evening and even if she had to swim out to the Pegasus, she was sure that Bart would listen to her. She would be able to warn him what he was up against and about the likelihood of some form of sabotage. Between them, they could check everything on board that could possibly be made unsafe, and Bart might have some idea about what the men were after.

Even if it were daytime, she wouldn't dare risk hitching a lift, not after what had happened. But how much of her dwindling cash could she afford to use? A sense of recklessness overcame her. She had to use whatever it took to get her to Bart's side. She wouldn't feel safe until she had done so.

Swallowing her fear, Gill asked the

bartender if he could recommend a taxi firm to take her to the Andaman Hotel.

'Ah, the Andaman, it very nice hotel, miss. You need nice taxi, yes?'

That probably meant expensive, Gill reflected.

'I . . . er . . . work there,' she offered by way of explanation. 'I haven't much money.'

'Then my brother, he will take you. He is very nice man. He has wife and children. You will be safe.'

Gill felt a sense of relief flow over her. 'Thank you.'

It was probably about ten minutes later when the taxi drew up outside the café and the driver tooted his horn. She was too keyed up to respond with much enthusiasm to the driver's chatter and he eventually fell silent, leaving Gill to her thoughts.

Would Bart be back at the Andaman before her? If so, would he give her the chance to explain? Would he believe her?

She glanced through the window. It

was dark outside now. They passed brightly-lit holiday complexes that she had viewed from the sea on the first sea cruise with Bart. Was it only two days ago? It seemed like a lifetime.

Why did she feel so strongly about Bart? She barely knew him, but, since when did that matter? She had taken to him straightaway, and he to her, she had felt. Besides, what was happening now had nothing to do with feelings. She feared for his safety, for his life, if his opponents had their way. Whatever happened in the next hour between her and Bart, she wanted to know that he was alive, even if she weren't with him.

When the taxi finally swung around a well-lit forecourt and pulled up outside an impressing Malaysian-style building, Gill knew the next hurdle was upon her — gaining entrance to the hotel. It was easier than she had dare hope for. A smiling porter opened the taxi door for her and she alighted with as much confidence as she could muster, bade her driver good-night and walked smartly through the entrance foyer to the reception area, where she was pleased to recognise the concierge on duty. He was smiling a welcome. Did that mean Bart wasn't back yet?

'Good evening, Miss Madison!'

Any surprise he felt by her unexpected arrival at the front of the hotel was carefully masked by his professional training.

'How may I help you?' he asked, with only a shade of anxiety in his voice. 'Has there been a problem with the cruise?'

Gill felt encouraged by his words. At least he hadn't been warned not to allow her over the threshold. She flashed him a brilliant smile.

'Nothing Mr Lawson couldn't handle. He had to put me ashore at Kuah and leave me to make my own way back overland. A minor problem, nothing to worry about. Has he returned yet, do you know?'

The man glanced at the clock.

'We expect them any time, Miss

Madison.' He indicated the seating area. 'Do you wish to await the return of the party over there? A drink, maybe, whilst you wait?'

With a wave of his left hand, he signalled to a waiter at the balcony bar that overlooked the swimming pool. Gill sank into the comfort of an easy chair, hoping that her nervous apprehension didn't show on her face as she awaited Bart's return. She eventually heard his voice before she saw him and quickly placed her glass of wine on to a tabletop as she rose to greet him. She wanted to run to him and fling herself into his arms and sob out her distress about Tiffany on to his shoulder but knew that she must control her emotion whilst they were in such a public place. So, she simply stood and hesitantly waited for him to notice her. His face was a picture and if the circumstances had been different, Gill would have laughed. As it was, her heart flared with hope as a flicker of delight lit his face, but it faded as swiftly as it came, replaced by a tightening of his facial muscles that made his expression quite fearsome. Gill took a hesitant step towards him, her lips framing his name.

'Bart, let me exp . . . '

With a quiet word to a member of his party to make sure everyone signed themselves in, Bart strode towards Gill, his expression grim. He grasped hold of her left arm and drew her forcibly farther away, out of earshot of other people.

'What are you playing at?' he hissed at her. 'Haven't you done enough damage without returning to do more?'

'Bart, I had to come!'

Her arm burned at his touch and even though his body bristled with anger, she felt a current of desire run through her. Her senses recognised that, behind his anger, his longing for her was as potent as hers for him. She grasped his upper arm with her free hand.

'You're in danger, Bart. I had to come to warn you.'

'Danger? What sort of danger? What trick are you planning now?'

His words hurt.

'It's not a trick, Bart. Tiffany has done something to your boat and . . . '

Her voice broke but she knew she had to go on.

'Tiffany's dead, Bart! She was murdered!'

Bart gripped both of her upper arms. 'What?'

'It's true, Bart. I overheard her talking to the man I've seen her with here. It began to rain and I saw them dash into a café so I followed them. They were seated at a table the other side of a screen and Tiffany said she'd put the laxative powder in the food yesterday,' she babbled, knowing she wasn't making much sense. However, Bart seemed to grasp the facts.

'But why?'

'I don't know! For some reason, they're trying to ruin your business. She wanted money off him and I followed them when they left the café. He led

164

her down a side street and . . . and shot her! Just like that, in cold blood!'

'Are you sure she's dead?'

He drew her into his arms as she nodded and hugged her close.

'What a shock for you! I can't believe it! What did you do? Did you talk to the police?'

Gill shook her head.

'I was too scared. I thought if he saw me there, he'd shoot me as well. He had run off before anyone got to the scene but I thought he might have been hanging around to see what happened. He must have put on a wig because he had long hair, but I recognised his voice. He was wearing dark spectacles, too. I doubt if anyone could describe what he looked like.'

Bart's face was sombre. He shook his head.

'I can't take it in. You're sure Tiffany's dead? Maybe she's just injured.'

'No, I could tell from people's expressions and someone took his jacket off and covered her face. There was nothing I could do for her and other people were nearer to the scene than I was, so I ran back to the main street where I felt safer and got a taxi to bring me back here.'

'But, why? Why should someone kill her?'

Bart's voice was taut with emotion. He shook his head, mystified.

'And what makes you think I'm in danger? If this man wanted to kill me, he's had ample opportunity if he's been staying here at the hotel.'

He thought of the bang on the head he'd received that first night on the beach.

'He could have killed me the other night instead of just knocking me out. Why didn't he?'

'I don't know. Maybe they didn't really want you dead, just out of the way. The man spoke of someone else with a boat.'

She thought back to the conversation she had overheard.

166

'A boat called the Pelican. He said, 'Dan can be getting the Pelican ready to come sailing out of the sunset!''

She stared at Bart's face. All colour had drained out of it and he seemed frozen in shock.

'What is it? What have I said?'

When he spoke, Bart's voice was no more than a whisper.

'My grandfather has a boat called the Pelican. He gave it to my cousin, Daniel, the same way he gave Pegasus to me.'

10

Gill stared at him for a few moments before she managed to stammer out, 'Your cousin?' in a weak whisper.

'Sounds preposterous, doesn't it? Even I am finding it hard to believe. There's no love lost between us but I didn't think he'd want to kill me.'

'Maybe he doesn't want to. Maybe the other man acted rashly on his own behalf when he killed Tiffany. I think she was sort of threatening to blackmail them if they didn't pay her for her efforts.'

'Maybe,' he agreed half-heartedly.

He brushed his hair back off his face. All fight seemed to have drained out of him. He heard his name called and turned towards Reception where the concièrge was waiting to speak to him. He pulled himself together.

'Let me deal with things here, Gill,

168

and then we'll get back to the boat and talk things through again. We'll say nothing to anyone here yet. I've got to think what to do. Did Tiffany say what she had done to Pegasus?'

Gill shook her head.

'No, just that she hoped it happened in a storm and that it would serve you right. Does that mean she has damaged the rigging or a sail?'

'Could be, though we often lower the sails during a storm and use the engine, but I don't see how she can have damaged the engine because we've used it today when we moored at Palua Payar jetty.'

Bart sighed heavily.

'I'll have to cancel all sea trips until I know everything is safe. Huh, it looks like my cousin has done enough already to put me out of business.'

The concièrge accepted Bart's apologetic cancellation of the sea trips until further notice and promised to pass on the information to the relevant hotel guests.

'I hope you get the problem sorted, Mr Lawson,' he added. 'There has been considerable interest shown in your programme of sea cruises, and another owner of a sea-going yacht has made enquiries about running sea trips from here. Naturally, we declined his introductory offer but may have to reconsider if your problems aren't sorted very soon.'

'Do you by any chance know the name of this other owner?' Bart asked.

'No, and I doubt if we would divulge confidential business matters to third parties.'

'No, of course not,' Bart agreed, 'but I appreciate your delay in replacing my business with any of my rivals as I rather suspect that my problems come from such a source. Would you at least let me know if any more approaches are made to you regarding the matter?'

Upon receiving the man's agreement, Bart returned to Gill's side.

'I can't do any more here. Let's get

back to the boat and talk over what we know.'

Even with Bart at her side, Gill felt very nervous as they left the lit corridors of the hotel and stepped outside into the warm jungle air. She clung closer to Bart than she would otherwise have done. The image of Tiffany lying crumpled in the roadway kept flashing across her mind and she knew she wouldn't feel easy until they were once more aboard Pegasus.

Even there, she couldn't relax. She hugged her knees to her body and tried to stop trembling. Wak joined them in the main cabin and they went over and over all that they knew.

'What does your cousin look like?' Gill asked when Bart was musing about Dan's possible involvement.

'He's about my height and build but has jet-black hair.'

'I think I saw him on my first visit to the hotel. He was talking to the man who killed Tiffany.'

Her voice was flat with sadness as her

words revived the memory of Tiffany's violent death. Bart reached out and squeezed her hand and the gesture brought some degree of comfort.

'We'll call at Kuah tomorrow and make enquiries at the police station,' he assured her. 'If you tell them that you saw her talking to this man here in the hotel, they will be able to find out who he is from the hotel registration, though I doubt if he will return here. As far as they know, I'm now on my own with Wak, and they will probably wait and see the effects of Tiffany's sabotage. We'll just have to check everything over as soon as it's light. And now, young lady, it's time to get to bed! You look done in. It's been a shocking day for you.'

Bart's voice was full of compassion for her and he drew her to her feet.

'I'm glad you came back,' he said softly, drawing her closer. 'Why did you? You could have just made your way off the island and out of danger.'

'I had to warn you because I care about you.'

Bart felt his heart lurch. Most of his anger against her was because his hopes of a relationship developing with her had been dashed to pieces. He felt his face soften and his body relax.

'I care about you, too,' he whispered. 'I wanted to believe you all along. I was angry with myself for being taken in.'

He saw a glimmer of hope begin to shine in her eyes. Her lips parted as she relaxed and he longed to kiss her again. Wak had left them alone but Bart sensed that it wasn't the right moment to indulge in a passionate embrace. The day's events stood between them, so he kissed her cheek lightly and turned her in the direction of her tiny cabin.

'Sleep well,' he whispered.

Not surprisingly, Gill's sleep was spattered with nightmare scenes of pursuit and bloodshed and she was relieved when streaks of light began to spread across the sky. Bart and Wak were already stirring and after a hasty breakfast of fruit and muesli they set to work examining the boat. Bart and Wak hoisted the sails and Wak swiftly shimmied up the masts to examine the fixtures and all the ropes. Bart examined the engine casing and investigated the gear mechanism.

Gill felt helpless to do much beyond looking for obvious things and even that left her at a disadvantage, as she didn't really know what was normal. She gave the toilet and washroom a good going over, making sure the intricate flushing mechanism hadn't been disabled.

'Right! Let's get over the side and examine the hull and propeller,' Bart commanded and he and Wak dived in together.

Gill spent the time cleaning the galley, even though it hadn't been used for food preparation the previous day, and made a list of things that needed to be replaced, such as muesli, coffee, dried milk and sugar, surprised that they had used so much of the latter.

'What about the dinghy?' Wak asked, when they climbed back on board, their task fruitless so far.

'We were using it when Tiffany was left alone on board,' Bart reminded him. 'She couldn't have tampered with that. All the dinghy might need is its tank refuelled. We may as well do it now. Get the fuel can, Gill. It's the small one under the seats over there. We need to refuel the main tank as well, when we go to Kuah. I should have done it yesterday but it won't matter. The spare can is full if we run out.'

Gill dragged out the smaller can, momentarily resting her left hand on a much larger fuel container at its side. When she withdrew her hand, she was aware that it was sticky and gritty and she frowned. She sniffed her hand but there was no smell of diesel fuel, so she tentatively touched the tip of her tongue to the grittiness. It tasted sweet. Sugar! Why should there be sugar on the fuel can?

'Fetch it over, Gill,' Bart's voice

called with a touch of impatience.

Gill straightened slowly, holding out the smaller can but looking intently at her left hand, her brain whirling as she recalled the moment of meeting Tiffany in the galley, surprisingly offering to make them a cup of coffee.

'What would happen if sugar were put in the fuel?' she asked.

'The engine would seize up and a right mess it would be to get it clean again. Why?'

He stepped closer, taking the small can out of Gill's hand. She pointed to the larger container still under the seating.

'There's some sugar on top of the can under there, around the opening. You can't see it but it's sticky to the touch.'

Bart touched it and tested the taste with his tongue.

'That's probably it!' he declared. 'I'd intended to refill the main tank if we'd gone on a cruise today. I only noticed how low the fuel was on our way back from Kuah. I wouldn't be surprised if Tiffany had siphoned some off. She certainly had the know-how. We could have been stranded anywhere out at sea, not very pleasant for the passengers, especially if there were children among them. Still,' he added, his face brightening, 'at least it shows that whatever Daniel's plans are, he doesn't actually intend to kill me, just to cause me enough annoyance and bad publicity to leave the area.'

He stared out to sea, his expression thoughtful.

'I wonder what he's up to, though? The Pelican is larger than Pegasus. He can do longer cruises with few passengers and still make more money than I can here. Does he just want it because I've got it? He was always that way inclined when we were kids and had holidays together with our grandparents. Always had to be the winner, the one on top!'

He turned to face Gill.

'Do you know what I feel inclined to

do when we get back from Kuah? I think we'll sail around the northern side of the island and see if we can spot him. He must be somewhere around if he's ready to arrive here and take over. Maybe, if we can talk, we'll be able to sort something out.'

Gill didn't feel happy with Bart's plan. The man she had caught a glimpse of her first day at the hotel didn't seem the sort to be filled with the milk of human kindness! But, maybe Bart knew him best, and he obviously wanted to sort out the rivalry with his cousin with no more unpleasant incidents.

'OK!' She shrugged. 'So, what's the plan? Do you want to return to the hotel and tell them we'll be back in business tomorrow?'

'No, I think we'd be best getting straight off to Kuah. The forecast was for an early downpour today. If we can get to Kuah before it comes, we'll be better equipped to outrun it on the way back.'

He put the small can back under the seat.

'We'd better save that in case we need it. Draw up the dinghy, Wak. We're about to up-anchor.'

Within minutes, Bart had started the main engine and was nosing Pegasus seaward. The air around them was still, the calm before the storm, Gill thought. Bart was hoping for more of a sea breeze once they had cleared the headland. There was some and Bart ordered the sails to be raised, immediately beginning to tack alternately to port and starboard to take advantage of the stronger side wind.

Gill marvelled at the ease with which Bart and Wak altered the set of the sails and felt the boat surge forward as the sails filled with wind, but it was a prolonged manoeuvre and it was obvious that they weren't making the headway Bart had hoped.

'I'm going to have to use the engine,' he called to Wak. 'Lower the sails.'

'There's a large yacht astern of us,'

Gill called. 'It seems to be heading our way.'

Bart shielded his eyes.

'It's the Pelican!' he announced shortly. 'It seems we're to have our confrontation sooner than I thought. We'll heave to and let them catch up with us. Daniel had better make this good.'

Leaving Wak to keep the catamaran nosing into the wind, Bart stood amidship, his legs braced against the ship's rail, waiting for the gap between the two vessels to close. The powerful yacht seemed to fly over the water. It made the catamaran seem small and clumsy by comparison. However, as the distance between the two boats rapidly narrowed, she began to feel alarmed. How was it going to stop in time?

Bart suddenly realised the same question and he turned and leaped towards the engine house.

'Start the engine! Pull hard to port!' he yelled to Wak.

Wak flicked the switch and the engine

burst into life. Bart had joined him in the confined space and they wrenched the wheel around. Gill clung to the mast as they swung around, just in time to avoid the larger vessel crashing into them amidship. Even so, there was only a narrow passage between them. Gill stared in terror at the cockpit where she fancied she could see the dark-haired man she presumed was Bart's cousin, but she wasn't one hundred per cent sure. It could have been anyone.

As the two vessels swung apart, Bart leaped out of the wheelhouse and up on to the cabin roof, shaking his fist at the retreating yacht and shouting some unintelligible words. His face was white as he looked down at Gill.

'I don't believe it! He tried to run us down! Has he lost control of his senses?'

'Bart! Bart!' Wak shouted, pointing out to sea. 'They are turning round. They are coming back.'

Bart and Gill stared in disbelief as the yacht swung in a wide circle and began to bear down on them again, this time with the wind behind it. The gap narrowed swiftly. Bart darted back into the wheelhouse and tried to guess which side to pull towards. If he turned too soon, whoever was at the wheel of the yacht would be able to follow them. If he left it too late, disaster was inevitable.

The yacht seemed to tower above them as it skimmed the waves towards them. Bart pulled to port, but he had guessed wrongly and the yacht followed. They almost made it. A few seconds earlier and they would have been clear. As it was, the knife-edge bow of the yacht caught the stern of the catamaran, whipping it round in a maelstrom of flying debris.

Partly up-ended by the force of the impact, the catamaran rocked violently. There wasn't time for any of the crew to do anything to save themselves. Gill saw Wak fall overboard in a graceful arc, and then the backwash of the yacht swept into them, tossing the catamaran over as if it were made of matchwood.

11

Gill felt herself falling, falling, down and down into the depths of the sea. Her ears roared with sound and her lungs felt as though they were burning. She spread out her hands to slow down her descent and kicked her feet, and felt herself rising. She looked upwards and could see the bright light of the sky getting brighter. She kicked harder, trying to reach the surface before her lungs burst. She desperately needed fresh oxygen.

'Hang on! Hang on!' she told herself, frantically kicking upwards.

She broke the surface and drew in great gulps of air, spluttering as seawater slapped against her. She trod water and looked around wildly.

'Bart! Bart!' she screamed.

Broken parts of the catamaran floated and bobbed on the surface. She grabbed hold of a piece and clung to it, letting it take her weight as she gasped in more air. Where were Bart and Wak? The sea was choppier than it had been and her vision was limited.

'Bart! Bart!' she screamed again.

As she rose on the crest of a wave, she saw the yacht circling the area. Were they looking for survivors with the intent of rescuing them, or to finish them off? She feared it would be the latter and was glad when she sank into a trough, safely out of sight for a moment. When she rose with the swell, she turned to look in the other direction and her heart leaped with joy. Bart was about twenty metres away, farther away from the yacht. His upper body was supported by part of the wreckage but she couldn't see any movement.

Gill looked round again. There was no sign of Wak. As she looked, the yacht sailed into her range of vision. They were coming back! If they rammed into

Bart, he wouldn't stand a chance of saving himself!

With no more thought, Gill abandoned her float and struck out towards Bart. When she reached him, she could see that he was conscious but had a deep gash on his head and blood was seeping out of it.

'Hold on!' she encouraged him.

There was more wreckage here. If she could manoeuvre Bart amongst it, they would be harder to spot from the yacht. With one hand on Bart's back and the other against his supporting float, she kicked as hard as she could and steered them into the midst of the wreckage.

The yacht was much closer now and was cutting through the waves like an arrow, its powerful engine sounding louder and louder as the distance between them closed. Gill was sure that no-one on deck could see them or even know for sure that they were there.

Bart's head and arms would be the most visible and so she shouted in his ear, 'Let go of the float. I'll hold you.

Relax! Trust me!'

The training she'd had in lifesaving whilst at college came back to her and she pulled him on top of her, taking firm hold under his upper arm with her right hand and grasping hold of his chin with her left. They were lower in the water now and she back-kicked towards the outer edge of the wreckage hoping that the yacht would be aimed at the middle. Her guess proved correct. The impact caused the wreckage to surge together and Gill feared they would be crushed, but the backwash split it apart again, leaving them once again in the open.

Which way would the yacht circle now? She was tiring and wouldn't be able to keep up this game of cat and mouse much longer. An explosive crack boomed over the sound of the waves. Gill looked around but couldn't see its source. The yacht had begun to turn once more towards them but now it veered away. She saw the sails rise swiftly and swell with wind and the

Pelican leaped forward, heading towards the open sea.

'They're going!'

Gill let go of Bart's right arm and grabbed hold of the nearest piece of wreckage.

'Can you hold on to it?' she yelled at Bart.

He grunted assent and she helped him raise his upper body on to the floating wreckage again. It was large enough to support her as well and she gratefully hauled herself on to it. As it rose with the next swell, she could see a speedboat coming their way and, in the distance, a large motor launch was in pursuit of the fleeing yacht.

Rescue was at hand!

Ten minutes later, wrapped in blankets, they huddled together in the well of the speedboat They had already learned that Wak had been picked up also and were delighted to see him also wrapped in a warm blanket Bart was recovering but still dazed by the blow to his head. Gill was just thankful that they had all survived.

Bart was aware enough to be able to tell her that they had been saved by the approach of a coastal patrol boat, whose occupants had witnessed the repeated attacks against the catamaran and its wreckage. There was little chance of the yacht evading capture, even if it outran the patrol boat as its identification had been noted and Daniel, as owner, would be held responsible, even if he tried to pretend that he hadn't been on board.

'But he's your cousin!' Gill said in bewilderment. 'Why would he try to kill you?'

Bart shrugged.

'From what our rescuer here has said, they suspect he's been drug-running. When Grandfather gave us each a boat, Daniel got first choice and chose the Pelican, so I got first choice of where to operate. I knew Daniel was put out when I chose Langkawi but I thought it was just his usual spite. He then said he would operate around

Eastern Malaysia and Thailand. I think he must have decided that access to the sea around Langkawi would give him a legal reason to be in this area as much as he wished without being under supervision.'

'What will happen to him when he's caught?'

'The penalty for any sort of drug trafficking in Malaysia and Thailand is the death penalty, even for people found with surprisingly small amounts,' Bart said flatly. 'With two possible deaths on his hands as well, I don't hold out much hope for him.'

They both fell into silent reflection for short while, until Gill asked, 'What about you? Your boat's gone. What will you do?'

And what about us, was in her thoughts. Was this to be the end of their time together? Wouldn't they be given the time to get to know each other properly?

She felt sad, not only about themselves but about Tiffany, a life carelessly wasted, destroyed. Bart was silent for a moment, as he, too, thought about the whole issue. Then he pushed that away and drew Gill closer.

'The boat was insured,' he mused. 'When Grandfather knows the whole story, I'm sure he'll let me have one of his other boats and possibly buy another to replace Pegasus. I rather fancy a Pegasus II. Of course, I'll have to get someone to crew with me, someone who knows all about boats,' he added.

Gill looked away sadly. He didn't want her then!

'And someone who can cook and clean, and be a regular Girl Friday.'

That was more like it!

'Er . . . have you anyone in mind?'

Bart grinned.

'I might contact an agency I know, or, on the other hand, I might just pull into Kuah and see who is sitting on the jetty, looking as though she had just missed the ferry to Penang and doesn't know what to do about it!'

Gill stared at him.

'You knew all along I wasn't from the agency?'

'I suspected as much, but I liked the look of you and wanted to get to know you, and I still do!' Bart looked at her hopefully. 'How about it?'

'Is that an offer of work?'

'Yes, if you can cope with a couple of weeks holidaying with me until I get things sorted out with Grandfather,' he added, smiling tenderly at her.

Gill nodded. 'That sounds wonderful.'

Bart drew an arm out of the blanket and tilted her face towards him.

'That's settled, then,' he said softly, before he turned her face upwards to kiss her.

THE END

Other titles in the
Linford Romance Library:

A FAMILY AFFAIR

Mel Vincent

When Harriet Maxwell, a divorced headteacher, spends the summer with her family in Spain, she falls in love with Carlos Mendoza: a widower with four children. But Harriet faces a dilemma: Zoe, her teenaged daughter, also falls for Carlos; the forthcoming marriage announcement cannot be made. Her predicament gets complicated when a misunderstanding prompts Carlos to leave. As Harriet copes with various family problems, and bonds with his children, she fears she will never see Carlos again.

LOVE IS A NEW WORLD

Helen Sharp

When Elizabeth Carleton met Jake Bartlett, Rolfe Sumner's farmhand, her life changed forever. Despite her thinking him as handsome, he was still a hired man. But in sleepy Washington, Vermont, Elizabeth found herself loving him, agreeing to marry him and becoming the owner of Sumner farm. And when she discovered Jake's dark secret, she fought to win him back from the edge of habitual bleakness — and won. For Liz, the summer she met Jake was the summer that changed her forever.